25⁰⁰
#4694

GREENHOUSE

It Will Happen in **1997**

GREENHOUSE

BY

DAKOTA JAMES

DIF

DONALD I. FINE, INC.

New York

Published in the United States of America by Donald I. Fine, Inc. and in Canada by Fitzhenry & Whiteside, Ltd.

Library of Congress Catalogue Card Number: 84-080788

ISBN: 0-917657-01-2

Manufactured in the United States of America

10 9 8 7 6 5 4 3 2 1

This book is printed on acid free paper. The paper in this book meets the guidelines for permanence and durability of the Committee on Production Guidelines for Book Longevity of the Council on Library Resources.

For Kathleen

CHAPTER 1

It was a hot day in February, almost ninety-five in the shade. Chicago was steaming. The sewer system had not been working right for most of the winter. A miasma of putrefying human waste and the oily stench of industrial pollutants drifted up through the city's manholes, mixed with the smell of decaying fish that hung over the lakeshore and spread downwind, toward the south and east, for miles.

Office air conditioners sputtered here and there about the city, even though it was against the law to turn one on. Power outages had been a problem for the last six months. So when Tom Puffit, sweating in his office on Wabash Avenue, received another of Casper Spent's memoranda, he hit the ceiling. "This loony bastard has got to go!" he bellowed to no one in particular.

The memo read:

February 10, 1997

To: Thomas Alvin Puffit, Dean
Freedom State University
School of Education

From: Casper Martin Spent, Assistant Professor

Re: My Place in Your Hi-Tech World

It has come to my attention that I was recently referred to, by a person or persons whose names I need not mention, as unworthy of being tenured as an associate professor. I am told I was called a "plaintive romantic out of touch with his times," "a disheveled wood duck," "a De Gaulle without the grandeur, only the nose and Adam's apple," and a "tree hugger who thinks we are going to Mars to plant flowering crabs."

I wish only to say this: the holy keep of my vision is not an absurd high-tech armory of rapacious schemes. It is not the lair of iron beasts that feed on arrogance and conceit. It is a primal world of fetus pulse and twitch, a world of sounds that drip, the very infancy of the soul. It is a strange and beautiful place, of sacred stones, of mysterious, moss covered glyphs, a place where cannibal passions rule, a place of temple ruins and unknown perfumes, a place of opal springs and ferns eternally wet with mist.

Each morning when I arise I enter that tabernacle on slippered feet. I clothe myself in priestly robes and move as softly as a shadow to its onyx altar. I unroll an ancient scroll made of light. I chant. Then I hide the scroll forever in my lanate sleeve of scarlet.

The memorandum was signed in Spent's usual way, with his initials and a small image of a unicorn.

Puffit knew what the unicorn meant. It was Spent's private symbol of deliverance. At the right moment, he'd once told Puffit at a cocktail party when both had their socks full, he would leap from obscurity to fame as nimbly as the unicorn leaps into the lap of virgins. It was all a matter of timing, Spent had said.

"Shit!" Dean Puffit muttered as he tossed the memorandum onto his secretary's desk. "The man is nuts. He's not just a different kind of hairpin. He's a fruitcake, off the wall... the ceiling, in fact. His mother must have been frightened by a loose chandelier. The president puts me on that new blue ribbon Commission on Public Information and those other lunatics as nutty as Spent turn on me. Now they're putting together some kind of national association. Going to put pickets up all over the damn place. That's what they're threatening. You know what one of their placards read yesterday when they were climbing over the fence around the University of Chicago Physics Research lab down on the southside? 'Ludditism with a human face.' Top that, Jen. Just try."

"What's Ludditism, dean?" Jennie Perch, his secretary, asked sheepishly.

"A Luddite was one of those nuts that wanted to break up machinery back in the eighteen hundreds 'cause they had no faith in the future. Loonies."

He slumped into one of the lounge chairs near her desk. "You know, Jen," he said, wiping his brow, "it's damn hard for a man to remain a futurist in times like this. The easy thing would be to give up, to turn into a goddamn doom-and-gloomer." He wiped his brow with a soggy handkerchief and stuffed it into his shirt pocket, then pulled the knot of his tie down. "But cool heads will prevail," he said. "You'll see." His arms dangled over the arms of the chair, his fingers combing whorls in the shag rug.

A mess it was, and hot. In 1992 carbon dioxide pollution of the earth's atmosphere had reached what weather scientists called the "tip-over point." The greenhouse effect was taking over, gathering momentum, turning the planet into a giant sauna.

There had been predictions for years that if pollution got worse something drastic would happen. Some said it would get hot, some said it would get cold. Some predicted a new ice age. That prediction was especially welcome to the snowmobile industry, which funded research that tried to prove it. And every time the weather took a brief, violent dip into the below-zero range it announced that the proof of its pudding was in the freezing. But those who predicted it would get hot were in the majority, and their ranks were infiltrated by fact-bound, no-growth fanatics.

Puffit figured that neither side could be trusted, which meant that he was free to think what felt most comforting—that nothing was really wrong. If the climate changed a few degrees one way or the other, so what? More problems meant more people hard at work solving them. Which meant high employment, higher income all around, more money for places like FSU. "A crisis may be what we need to get this damn economy moving," he'd said just last week at a meeting of the other deans in the chancellor's office. And he repeated what had become something of a maxim for him: "More problems, more people working to solve problems."

The people of the United States reacted to the crisis the way a great people could be expected to react, with a mixture of bewilderment, name calling, catatonic aplomb within the conservative community, sarcastic wit within the liberal community, and in the high-tech community the morbid conceit of a haughty aristocrat about to blow his brains out with an heirloom dueling pistol.

In New York a musical called *Ooops* played to the biggest crowds in the history of show business. It drew people from all across the northern tier of states, from as far away as Montana. People living closer to New York, in Philadelphia, Baltimore and Boston, saw the show three and four times.

The theater where *Ooops* was playing was as hot, fetid and fuliginous as a Port Said men's room. But the crowds responded with grace and ingenuity. They went to the show in underpants and undershirts. The dress quickly turned into a fashion craze, the Kowalski look.

The hero of *Ooops* was a power-wielding grain speculator, Winston Gain, who moved to Moose Jaw when drought ended American wheat farming. He cornered the Canadian market and suddenly, inadvertently (hence *Ooops*) became the man to see in world capitals, including Moscow. And equally suddenly and inadvertently (because of a sarcastic wager with his pampered wife) he mounted a worldwide program of ideological reform. It started with a ten-point program for the "privatization of communism," which was immediately heralded by starving Soviets as "the final flower of Marxist-Leninist realism." Massive land reform followed. Gain forced every nation that imported his wheat—which included most—to redistribute all arable land to the jaded, landless aristocrats found huddling on yachts off Majorca. He called the redistribution scheme "progressive feudalism."

The showstopper of *Ooops* was a rollicking rondo, the lyrics of which were taken from the writings of M. Stanton Evans, Roscoe Drummond and Paul Harvey. The final line from the booming chorus was a mighty "Goooooood Daayee!"

Southerners did not take to *Ooops* with the enthusiasm of northerners. Their public transportation system had broken down three years earlier, amidst the bangs and sizzles of exploding Greyhound bus tires on scorching highways. Airport traffic was down eighty percent in places like Atlanta. Dixie politicians were not amused: "Time the damned Watthouse did something about that thar goddamned greenhouse effect." But little changed, except for the worse. From the Texas Panhandle to the peanut country of Georgia, the countryside was burning up, turning slowly but inexorably into desert.

Northward from Texas the humor had pretty well gone out of the line about there being "nothin' between the Panhandle and North Dakota 'cept a barbed wire fence." All the way to Minot sand dunes began to appear, first as long brownish swatches of wind-drifted dirt, then as rippled ridges of tan dust, finally as great, starkly beautiful billows of high quality sand. Now and then ferocious squall line storms would sweep across the plains. They were as brief as they were fierce. Little rain soaked in and all it meant was that the gullies got deeper and the washes grew wider.

During the late 1980s irrigation in the Great Plains had begun to peter out. The vast reservoir of "fossil water" that had been trapped beneath the plains a million years ago in the giant Ogallala aquifer were pretty well played out, and since that water was nonrenewable, prairie farming and ranching went downhill fast. Here and there a solitary pumping station could still be seen, with small herds of ornery beef cattle pushing and shoving at water troughs under the eyes of sullen cowboys with electric cattle prods. But that was about it. About the only thing the lonely ranch hand lived for during a long day in a blistering saddle was his single evening bottle of beer in the bunkhouse. The price of fresh water had driven the price of beer up to where it cost a man a day's labor to buy a single bottle.

When they could travel, southerners headed east or south, to the ocean. There they huddled like swarms of irritable lemmings, cursing Yankee indifference as they hoarded supplies of talcum powder.

A few good old boys were able to turn the crisis to advantage. They established a "condoraft" industry, mass producing cheap, two-family trailerhouses that could be mounted on tractor-tire inner tubes bought for a song from ruined cotton and peanut farmers. All along the lee sides of the Carolina outer banks and the inland waterway of Texas and Louisiana, schools of condorafts began to appear like great clusters of Hong Kong junks. Their owners survived largely on fish and a few insisted that they at last were living the good life they foresaw before retirement.

Most of Florida south of the Panhandle was abandoned, except for a few diehard developers frantically bulldozing what remained of Florida's citrus country in hope that the housing industry depression would bottom out, then be followed by a boom. If they could hold out, they figured, they would make a killing.

In the early 1990s southerners with real money, the kind who had had enough sense to invest in gold, and wealthy northerners used to wintering in Florida had begun to flee the sunshine states for Canada and Alaska. The Yukon town of Dawson had, in fact, become a new jet-set watering hole.

Many northerners adjusted to the heat rather well. In the Lake of the Woods country of northern Minnesota people gamboled about during the winter months in golf shirts, shorts and jogging shoes. On the Alaskan tundra bowling on the green had become all the rage and, despite a boom in the black fly population, a crotchless short-short styled by a high fashion Parisian designer became the thing to be seen in in Nome.

To be sure, a pall of anxiety hung over the pleasures of the north. There continued to be predictions that the warming trend would continue. Scientists were beginning to suspect that the sudden extinction of migratory birds was evidence that something might be wrong. And when the Alaskan and Canadian caribou herds died off, the American Association for the Advancement of Science passed a unanimous resolution calling for more research, massive federally funded projects, to study sun spots and galactic gases in particular. Perhaps the trouble was in the sun or the stars.

The governor of Alaska took events in stride. "Small enough price to pay for progress up here in the north," he announced boldly. "We have every intention of building a thriving tourist industry on the beaches of Kodiak Island. Honolulu, move aside! Eskimo girls in hula skirts? Yessir. You better believe it."

Off the record he expressed a different view. The hordes of sweating American sunbelters that were coming ashore, mostly at night, on the southern coast of his state bothered him. He knew that swarms of perspiring Mexicans could not be far behind. The Rio Grande wall had not stopped the Mexican migrations. "I can take some of them," he confided to his wife, "but them swaggering Texans and hangdog greasers are one hell of a price to pay for Alaska catchin' up with the lower forty-eight." Most Eskimos agreed with him.

Back in the late eighties there had been plans to solve the drought problem worldwide, once and for all. A consortium of nations, the United States, the USSR, Japan and Norway had contracted for a feasibility study for a colossal project that would pump out Lakes Superior, Michigan, Baikal, Victoria and Titicaca and push water in giant pipelines to the edges of encroaching desert.

The Hudson Center, at Croton-on-Hudson in New York State, did the study. Their report was a hefty, upbeat volume of six hundred pages called *World Water Unlimited*. But the water report had been on the streets for only six months when calamity struck. The west Antarctic ice sheet abruptly began to melt. Some unknown "tip-over" factor there, too, had begun to take effect. Little America disappeared into the sea. Suddenly Bangladesh was largely under water as well as most of the plains provinces of South

Vietnam. At Rotterdam and Baltimore engineers were frantically trying to raise their docks and heavy equipment above the flood by hammering great long pilings into the ocean floor, then hoisting the docks and equipment above the tide.

The United Nations assembly erupted in a torrent of insult and counterinsult as the water levels rose. "This report is not humorous reading, gentlemen!" shouted the small, suitcase-colored ambassador from Bangladesh. "It is optimistic, but it is not humorous!" '*World Water Unlimited*—the key to a bright blue world of tomorrow.' What rubbish! Today, gentlemen and ladies, my country, one of the less developed countries, one of the truly *great* LDCs, is under water... Or most of it, anyway. We of Bangladesh do not need to wait for tomorrow. We are drowning today. The proud people of my land must tread water from sunup to sundown and share space on floating debris. We survive on rice and wheat-mush handouts pressed into our mouths from bureaucrats floating about on US AID launches. It is a despicable situation! The rich ride about in launches while the poor tread water until they sink!"

The British delegate coughed loudly, then interrupted the man from Bangladesh. "Sir," he said, "might I suggest that you immediately instruct your people to take shelter on the upper floors of their homes."

A Pakistani delegate watching the Bangladesh delegate smiled sarcastically, then poked an elbow into the Sri Lankan delegate next to him. "Is the man's country underwater or underdeveloped? Surely he could be more precise."

"More IUDs and we'd have fewer damned LDCs," the Swedish delegate next to the Sri Lankan mumbled.

The debate swirled on. A Kenyan wanted to know if the United Nations would be prepared to fund glass-bottomed boats for those nations whose great seacoast cities were disappearing under water. "I am fervently convinced," he said in an emotional speech, "that the answer to many of these problems is tourism. My best guesstimate (he loved the word *guesstimate*) is that tourists would flock to view cities beneath the sea. There is something beautiful and romantic about that sort of thing. The story of Atlantis has captivated our imaginations for a thousand years. I, for one, would dearly love to view Venice through the bottom of a boat. My guesstimate is that many others would share my desire."

The Kenyan's optimistic attitude did not go unnoticed by Dr. Simone, the ambassador from the United States, a former professor of economics from Urbana. Simone had been sitting in his assembly chair for weeks, submitting stoically to the pummeling of Third World critics. His instructions were to say nothing if he could not say something positive about the catastrophe engulfing the planet.

The following day Simone delivered a carefully worded statement to the assembly. "Gentlemen and ladies, ambassadors, representatives," he began. Pessimism is a frame of mind, not an economic model. The temporary abundance of water causing difficulty in some LDCs must be met boldly. I am calling for a game plan that includes the immediate building of enlarged port facilities in the LDCs, as well as in the DCs. The present abundance of water calls for vision. The famed Northwest Passage will soon be free of ice year-round, open to vessels of trade, to tankers large and small, to junks and dhows and barges. Where once the clumsy polar bear stalked, frightening Eskimo children, cities will rise, grand cities, climate-controlled beneath great Buckminster Fuller domes. They will be heated by laser beams from satellites. The satellites needed to get the job done are coming on line at this very moment, at the same time that we of the American government have put a new game plan in place. We of the world community may have our differences, but I say, build ports. For God's sake, build more ports!"

President Kempt had picked the UN ambassador when he had been shown a *Chicago Tribune* letter to the editor by Simone. The letter, featured on the front page of the *Tribune,* was a scathing retort to environmentalists deploring the extinction of migratory birds. The letter began, "So our feathered friends won't be around to freeload any longer. Big deal." It went on to cite the cost of birdseed set out by backyard bird-watchers. The figure was substantial. "Were that same money put to productive use in properly diversified investment portfolios, the earnings would double in five years and quadruple in ten, and by the year 2030 provide a handsome nest egg for every man, woman and child under thirty years of age."

It was the kind of thinking Kempt intended to push in his "New Surge Conservatism." The bottom line of his new game plan called for supply-side sacrifice on a scale no president had ever had nerve enough to propose.

Kempt was shrewd: He capitalized on the fact that the atomic bomb problem had finally become a very real pocketbook issue. A hundred thousand atomic warheads were stored about the planet, tiny, deadly, unseen glowworms of death, in tunnels, bunkers, salt mines, vaults and ramshackle waterfront warehouses in some of the more advanced LDCs. The cost of storing the warheads was racing ahead of the benefits of storing them. When an internationally sponsored study of storage costs hit world headlines people in every country were infuriated. It turned out that in the United States alone it took more money to store warheads than to store the vast hoard of American grain, butter and cheese through all of the 1970s and '80s. "The situation has become impossible," said a congressman from

Utah on the floor of the House. "It's time to bring some common sense to bear on this issue. Either use the damn things or get rid of them!"

Then an atomic power plant meltdown occurred on the Rhône, drenching the valley with plutonium. Two hundred thousand Frenchmen, mostly socialist winery workers, and an equal number of barrels of fine cabernet were contaminated. As the Frenchmen began to die and the wine began to go flat the French government sought to allay public anxiety by assuring its people that the half-life of the radioactive pollutants was two thousand years, not twenty thousand years as its political critics claimed. The facts seemed to make little difference; the socialists were booted out of office in a landslide.

The mounting resentment against the kind of left-wing nonsense that had brought France to grief was not lost on the American electorate. Their politics veered sharply to the right and further strengthened Kempt's hand. He moved boldly. He proposed to export more than half of the atomic warheads on hand to LDCs for use in atomic power plants. Experts from the American atomic energy industry would be sent to the LDCs to assure that their new atomic industries would operate as smoothly as they had in the United States. It was the kind of supply-side thinking that the industrial community loved, and they supported it wholeheartedly.

The president also struck a sympathetic note among the movers and shakers when he announced in a press conference that he thought President Reagan had been much too timid in attacking the problem of industrial raw materials. The industrial world, he observed, was hostage to miners of scarce metals like tungsten, beryllium and cobalt, miners who had fallen under the influence of hostile leftist governments of the Third World. Some of these governments were radical in the extreme, rejecting the very idea of progress itself, including the opportunities it provided to thousands of workers to spend their lives in the dark digging mile-long holes. The American people, said Kempt, would have to come to grips with reality. That reality included exhaustion of domestic supplies of minerals mined outside the public park system. Americans loved those parks, but it was time for sacrifice. He was asking the people to surrender their traditional idea of a park. Yosemite, the Grand Tetons, Glacier and McKinley were all suspected of containing rare metals critical to high technology. Barring a groundswell of opinion to the contrary, he said, they would be mined.

For a time, Kempt proved to be right. The park mines produced sufficient riches to fuel American high technology for over two years before they began to peter out.

Kempt put another imaginative game plan in place for use of the devastated national parks. Amidst the great tailings in Yosemite, the Tetons and Glacier Park (McKinley Park in Alaska proved to be a dry hole), Kempt's secretary of the interior, a disciple of President Reagan's renowned James Watt and a man who shared Watt's conviction that the earth was given to man to use up, quickly established a new park concept. It called for "moonscape wonder parks" to be built amidst the wastelands and blast debris. Soon hiking trails, narrow gauge trains and special "astronaut rides," complete with spacesuit apparel for rent, crisscrossed the mighty desolations. "Relive the heroic age of the moon explorers!" blared speakers above the ticket sale booths.

The moonscape wonder parks were a smashing success. Mobs flocked to them from everywhere across the country, people of all ages, races, creeds. Off-road vehicle owners in particular were deliriously happy tearing up and down the great mountains of tailings and along the muddy beds of former trout streams. Here at last, they cried, was the kind of park that the average working-class American loved and was willing to fight for.

But there continued to be talk of the need to "ratchet down the American lifestyle," even within Kempt's cabinet. The mounting concern over the greenhouse effect gave the argument increasing credibility. And the sudden failure of the rare-metal mining game plan pushed the whole thing into the public consciousness more rapidly than expected. But on the whole, public confidence remained pretty steady. It was shaken, largely in the Sunbelt, because of drought, desert and unremitting sticky heat. The heat was not in Kempt's game plan, and he had not intended to put it in place.

In the north, things began to ratchet down when the high-tech magnetic levitation rail system that the free-spending liberals had built faltered. The trains depended heavily on alloys that used rare metals. Within months, Chicago found its new "Fastram" mag-lev commuter system stalled. The governor had to declare a state of emergency while ancient, rickety South Shore commuter coaches were hauled out of their graveyard at Michigan City, given a coat of aluminum paint (some with yellow trim as a boost to rider morale), and put into service. The same was done with the antique cars rotting in the yards of the old Illinois Central line. Where the overhead trolley cables had rusted and fallen they were propped up by telephone poles and wired or welded into place. Soon the cars, with their square wooden-framed windows and wicker seats, were sputtering and clanking along at thirty, sometimes forty miles an hour, their trolley wheels up top sputtering and sparking as they drew power from high voltage lines, the power itself surging in from two atomic power plants still in operation fifty miles to the west.

When the system went back into service, the governor of Illinois gave a speech at the ribbon-cutting ceremony at the Indiana-Illinois border. He chose as his theme a line from James Whitcomb Riley. A tribute, he'd said, to his Hoosier colleague who had come all the way up from Indianapolis for the occasion. "Takes a heap of livin' to make a house a home," he quoted.

The relevance of the line to the debacle of the mag-lev system was pretty well lost on his audience of transportation officials and experts. Their attention was on the recently inaugurated "People Mover System," a fleet of canvas-topped army trucks, each appointed with rows of wooden benches, operating in and out of the Chicago metropolitan area. The director of operations on the new PMS periodically moved back from the small cluster of people listening to the speeches to take a message from the dispatcher on his army field radio. When cost of petroleum doubled again early in July the new People Mover System was swamped with customers. The governor's speech left the director bewildered, too. "Don't get it," he said to a subordinate. "Who in hell is this Riley? Sounds like a rube to me. Besides, it's too goddamned hot to stand around and be philosophical. I got potholes on that damn interstate to worry about. Lost axles on three trucks in one week in those suckers."

CHAPTER 2

For Spent, life on the trains had become a crucifixion. In the morning, on the way into town, he felt as if he had joined a band of demented fools setting out to colonize a brackish swamp of tedium. Strangers exchanged the desperate glances of horse thieves being readied for the gibbet. Friends smiled small, defeated smiles or babbled needlessly... Some heartless boss was taking it out on them because the windows in the Chicago skyscrapers were not designed to open. Or some secretary was in a pout because someone had made off with the electric fan.

In the evening the whole thing ran in reverse, like a clock gone mad from the sound of its own remorseless ticking. Sweating passengers crammed into the cars, then jiggled along, mile after mile, fermenting. Their spray-on deodorants gave the car the odor of a rancid bouquet of violets. It reminded Spent of the purple eyelids of an aging actress he once dated. And every few nights the train was hours late. Passengers rode past Gary in the dark, like miners who spent their days in perpetual gloom, tunneling from purgatory to hell and back again.

Spent sprawled, one foot in the aisle, in the third seat of the second car. Good grief, he thought, I'm pushing forty-five. I'm growing old. I'm approaching God on a numbed rump. He threw his head back and stared at the ceiling.

But it had not always been that way. Six years earlier, when Spent thought his book, *Ruling Equations,* which was intended to update Paillot de Montabert's great romantic statement on "visual vocabularies attending great agitations of the soul" was sold, he traveled in midwinter, on a whim, to Sacramento to celebrate. He knew no one there, but he liked the name *Sacramento.* In his journal he rhapsodized:

> My plane flies at thirty-five thousand feet. In this grand, encapsulated moment, I escape the stagnating world below by force of whirling winds and fire, in a metal creature of godlike power, on silvered wings, a gleaming arrow. And as we fly over the great plains of Nebraska, the endless patterns of snow-blown wheatfields asleep, giant rectangles of slumbering fallow, giant lozenge shapes of soil, a mysterious color-famished world of insinuating tones, then a thousand, small gray waterholes frozen deep, I sing inside. And as we approach the snow-topped mountains of the Great Divide, a magnificent white wall booming down the continent, the plan for release of my imprisoned spirit takes its shape. I entertain the unicorn. I trace the daring blueprint of a new life. I've put it all in the *Equations.*
>
> I love great heights. I think more boldly when I am high. So with this third scotch everything seems right, the haze hovering above lands to the north, over my shoulder to the right, where Custer stood, tall, Nordic and unafraid, as he blazed away at pagans, the sunlight ricocheting off the wing, the fit of the elegant, sale-priced stretch socks snug about my shins. I think of

everything: the cause of prairie shadows, a painting I once saw of a Carolingian king (his crown was of beaten gold and red enamel), the well-known fear of pain in second-rate poets, the scarcity of piety in the pious, the ingrown-toenail minds of literary critics. I hear everything: the soft, conspiring whisper of the air vents, the small, metallic echo of the miniature conversation across the aisle, the rattle of the lunch trays in the galley, the voices of the stewardesses as they work and play like cats and kittens.

Crossing Carson's Sink the captain greets us on the intercom and tells us where we are. He speaks in a lumbering Stetson drawl, in a voice you'd hear around the jousting sheds at Camelot. Then my mind sweeps down to the land below. I think of creatures long extinct, of ponderous dinosaurs, thick-skinned, greenish, with toothy grins, as convinced of immortality as any oaf in the society of men. I think of great birds with leather wings, buried in rust-flecked sediment, turned to salt and stone.

Then my mind is lifted on updrafts of splendid inspirations to the mountain timberline where the air is as thin as the breath of ghosts, to distant umber cliffs where falcons roost, their shoulders hunched under feathered capes of crimson. They sit, poised like judgment day, against the pale blue of the eternal sky. Their diamond eyes are daggers, piercing canyons a half mile deep. I see rivulets of quicksilver forming in the mountain snow, becoming gentle, gelid brooks, then rivers thundering downward over granite boulders, frothing, glorying in the fierce demands of gravity, flooding toward small and lonely lakes that lie high upon lordly, cerulean plateaus, contemplative, reflecting the bowl of heaven, beatified by the stillness of their magnificent isolation.

I remember the days when white-haired hermits and solitary prospectors, their minds aglow with gold, roamed the wilderness like tawny panthers, savoring the life of the recluse, moving soundlessly in forested canyons, bound only by the pulse of seasons, muffled in the solitude of moon-glazed nights, suspended among ancestral shadows, timeless fellows held in thrall like the grizzly bear by the sacred monotony of the wilds. I see them curled round their fires at night, listening to a distant heron's cry and the hiss of the green aspen log burning slowly through the darkened hours, men asleep among the dreams of man's wild childhood, until morning glows in eastern evergreens. I see them waking, rubbing wise old eyes as the dawn's first bold moment comes, shattering bolts of yellow light against the western canyon cliffs. Red darts and finches flash. The canyon walls ring with song. Another boisterous celebration of the sun begins. I see the morning's crystal light rout the fears secluded in those lonely hearts. In the chill of dawn, courage and loneliness and joy are one.

I think of an old mountain man asleep down there, high in some windswept pass, lost, wrapped in moss and time, icicles afire in his hair, and a glorious tintinnabulation frozen in his head.

But when Spent got the manuscript for *Ruling Equations* back from the publisher, an editor had penned a single comment at the bottom of the first page. "This is good, but not good enough to encourage."

"Life is a brief candle, all right," Spent wrote in his journal that day. "But mine cannot be lit. An envious pipsqueak editor has given it a wire wick."

When Spent got to Tremont that night he did not go directly home. He hiked the half mile to Lake Michigan. The moon had risen in the early evening light, but the lake was not the softly burnished plaque of Prussian blue he had watched so often on other moonlit nights, heat-lightning playing among the clouds far to the west. The wind from the north was up. Breakers pounded the distant sandbars; swells formed a half mile out from land and drove toward Spent in great belligerent heaps. They grew huge white paws of fury, lunged forward, collapsed, mauling the shallows, then slithered on their bellies toward him and, sighing with fatigue, sank into the sand.

He retreated inland to the high dunes and sat among the clumps of saw grass. Thoughts of home tumbled over him. He thought of his father working part-time as a janitor in the white, shiplap village hall.

It seemed that his father never really held a full-time job and for that his mother would bawl Harry out. "If you'd stop drinking up every penny we make things wouldn't be so bad! You're a souse, Harry, nothin' but a souse." And his father would grumble about the tyranny of living with a hatchet head and stride defiantly to the tavern to get even again.

Once his mother called Harry a souse during a quilting bee at their house. Spent had witnessed that strange, primal scene. Harry had come into the front room where the women sat around the quilting frame doing their stitching as they talked about one another's ailments—the adhesions that could develop following removal of a gallbladder, the dangers of a sour stomach, the death of the old lady living to the west near the village of Cumberland. She had been too proud to allow herself to pass gas in the presence of nurses at the hospital. She had puffed up somewhere inside and finally burst a seam.

Harry's eyes sparkled from too much beer. He tried to tell a joke about a woman who forgot to button up the seat of her husband's long johns hanging on the clothesline. His wife cut him off. "Harry, take your stupid jokes somewhere else, you *souse.*"

He was hurt, incensed. Tilting forward on his toes he said, "I won't put up with your insults again, Mabel. You've insulted me in front of our friends for the last time!"

"Puttin' your foot down, you *souse?"*

Harry steadied himself on the door jamb. "I'd rather be dead than put up with your insults!"

"It's your decision, Harry," she answered. "Now, leave us alone. We're busy."

"Well," he'd said with a huff. "If that's the way you want it..." And Harry marched down into the basement and brought up a tin of the Paris green insecticide he used to kill potato bugs in their little garden. He strode into the front room, took a handful of the dust and stuffed it into his mouth. But it was dry and he gagged and coughed, spewing a cloud of dust across the room. He turned and ran for the door, coughing violently.

"You clumsy, stupid, skinny little fool!" his mother shouted from the door. "Who's gonna clean that quilt now? You?" As he wobbled about, still coughing, she kicked him in the seat of the pants.

"This ain't the only way, Mabel," he sputtered. "I got other ways to kill myself. I got a good imagination, Mabel, and *don't* you forget it." Finally his coughing subsided.

"Well then, Harry, use your imagination! But now you rinse that big mouth of yours out with water. I don't want you complaining about your stomach for a week."

"I'm going to show you, Mabel! By Christ I will!"

"Don't you bring the Lord into this, you *souse."*

Harry followed her into the house and to the sink. As he stood there rinsing his mouth, he glared at her. "Over in the outhouse behind that village hall is a *rope*. I'll tie it around my neck and loop it over a peg and sit. My weight will kill me. I ain't as skinny as you think. And you'll have a lot of explaining to do to our friends, Mabel. A *hell* of a lot of explaining."

She shoved him toward the door. "Well, toddle over there right now. I'll have one of the ladies go over and cut you down as soon's our quilt is done and we had our coffee and cake." She went back to the living room where the quilt frame had been tipped on its side and the Paris green dust was being brushed off.

Harry took the boy of seven and went to Jack Kodesh's tavern. As Casper sat on the barstool next to him Harry smoothed down six glasses of beer. "A bit green around the gills there, Harry," Kodesh had remarked.

"Off my feed a bit," Casper's father had replied.

Sometimes their visits to the tavern took two or three hours and Casper would lose count of Harry's beers. But he would sit quietly next to his father, his elbows sprawled out on the bar in front of him—his body was gangly even at the age of seven—answering Harry's friends in monosyllables. But he took it all in, stories of deer hunting, epic encounters of town braggarts, the beauty of the tiny necklaces of bubbles streaming upward in Harry's salted glass of beer, the strong fishy odor of the Blind Robbins his father often ate. They were cellophane-wrapped smoked herring, deep brown in color, almost black, and marvelously perdurable in the mouth. And Casper's own delicious bottle of cream soda, as tasty after the fizz had been swirled out of it as when Kodesh had first removed the cap. It paid, Spent learned, to be a patient observer. Later in life he would agree wholeheartedly with Dr. Johnson that nothing has given man as much happiness as his taverns.

There was a pragmatic quality in his wife that Harry found coarse and unattractive. He realized it suddenly the first night of their honeymoon when she refused to take off all her clothes when they went to bed. It was not a matter of modesty, just too much fuss, she said. She seemed to view sex as an exercise in traffic management. "Here, Harry, not there, for heaven's sake." "Now get to the point, Harry." Soon he suggested they sleep in separate beds. He would retire late and sit up in bed reading Zane Grey.

Spent's mother's practicality was the reason Spent got a sled, one of the few real toys he ever owned. She had told the town blacksmith, a kindly old man named Anderson, "I want nothin' flimsy. We ain't puttin' hard-earned money on somethin' that ain't solid." So she supervised the sled's construction, walking over to the blacksmith's shop twice a day.

On Christmas Eve, under the tree, it did not look at all like a sled to Casper. It was big, heavy, stiff as a plank, with heavy oaken runners. It was painted red. Casper secretly dubbed it the "red moose," and he hid it in the woodshed, only pretending to use it. But his mother found the sled hidden beneath a pile of firewood and told him he was an ungrateful, selfish little boy. "You go play with Louie and Bobby," she said, "and don't forget I can see that hill from my window. You enjoy yourself or I'll give you something to really think about."

Bobby had a Flexible Flyer. He would slam and scoot, laughing, past Casper, then hook the Moose with his toe and send it careening into the ditch, always into the same clump of sumac. Casper would untangle the Moose's horns from the brush and then lug it back to the top of the hill. The Moose was heavy and stubborn as a log.

Casper tried alchemy, trying to make a game of his humiliation. He told Bobby and Louie he would be a dirigible and they could be planes and shoot him down. Still, he found crashing tiresome.

Once he tried to use Louie's sled but it was too small. And Bobby would never let him use the Flexible Flyer. So Casper spent most of his time sitting on the Moose at the top of the hill watching Bobby and Louie, laughing as much as he could. But he often thought of killing Bobby, of stuffing him with Paris green.

* * *

Spent walked home some time after midnight. The night had grown very quiet. The dog penned behind Kunst's tavern let out a howl. Toward the south on Highway 12 a truck moaned toward the east. He wondered if it were not a secret unmarked machine, part of a caravan laden with dead from some hit in South Chicago.

When he went to bed he didn't immediately fall asleep. He sat up in bed and took a couple of reassuring swipes at his private fifth of Canadian Club. Then he lay back and closed his eyes. There was a buzzing in his ears. He would, he thought, let the angels speak to him. He smiled as he asked, "Is this the rustle of their wings, or the soft purr of my hypertension?"

At 2:30 Spent woke up with a sour stomach. He put an end to it decisively with four Rolaids and a spoonful of Maalox. Then he propped his pillows and read a short story from the 1920s. It was about a German U-boat captain who fell in love with a beautiful captive from a luxury liner he sank. The captain and his lady led a mutiny on the U-boat and the entire crew joined their cause. They sailed to a lovely island in an estuary of the Niger. They went completely native, surviving on palm hearts and roast pig. They established their own religion, a special kind of ancestor worship. In secret ballot they picked Pancho Villa as their Zeus.

"Once again," he said to himself as he dozed off, "the comely form of an aesthetic triumph will see me through this haunted night."

CHAPTER 3

Spent knew his memorandum struck home the minute he hung up his office phone. Puffit's secretary had called to say that the dean would like to join him at Cirroco's for lunch.

It was the first sign of a break that had come Spent's way in ages. His career at Freedom State had been anything but exciting. Most of the time it was dull or depressing, if not humiliating. Nothing he wrote was accepted anywhere. Publishers routinely returned his essays with no comment, or some vaguely worded insult. *Ruling Equations* gathered dust in his file cabinet. His large novel was returned from a Boston publisher with a hurtful little note calling his style "epispastic, as well as dated." It was the same thing with his work as an inventor. The Chicago firm that specialized in winter clothing found his idea for clip-on heel spikes for pedestrians skidding about on icy streets unfeasible, "now that the weatherman has abolished winter."

Spent came to FSU a year after it opened, from one of the small satellite campuses of the University of Wisconsin system. When he first saw Freedom State he was not completely impressed. Four thirty-story concrete high rises anchored the corners of a massive plaza, the Plaza of Inspirations, that formed the core of the campus. The buildings were gloomy, soot-stained and grimly monotonous. The plaza was a slab of concrete, its cracks and fissures patched with blacktop. Here and there a few small trees clung to life, abused by vandals and on the verge of suffocation in the polluted air.

Freedom State University was founded in 1989. Though it was part of the state university system, it was built entirely with federal money, during one of the great swings of the political pendulum. It was proof, said Chicago liberals, that their representatives in Washington cared about public higher education. In fact, its establishment was the first act of the liberal presidency following a backlash against miserly conservative rule. The campus went up almost overnight, on a massive tract of land freed up in the Chicago Loop by a group of gung-ho developers with impressive connections in the right places. They dynamited five blocks of old office buildings—several of which had been mysteriously burned a year earlier—to the ground and then went broke.

Spent sat, bemused, on a bench at one corner of the enormous plaza. "I have seen the future," he thought, "and it's made of dirty concrete." But later in the day, after a successful interview, when he saw the university's mission statement boldly engraved on a bronze plaque mortared into the corner of the administration building, his eyes filled with tears. It read:

> Freedom State University's mission is to provide the new American education to all, male and female, red, black, brown, yellow or white, endowed with the gifts of nature or deprived of them by dialectic caprice,

> driven by winds of high ambition or becalmed by sloth, for persons possessing tendencies or not, yearning only for a better tomorrow, preferably with full and gracious subsidy.

Over the next seven years things changed for Spent. He began to suspect that the university was not the "peak of excellence" its founders prophesied, but a miserable populist sump. And in one of his early memoranda of conscience to Puffit he called it a place where "anybody with any sense of quality at all will quickly succumb to backwater fever."

Spent's attitude cost him. When his promotion papers came before the Tenure Recommendations Committee for the first time, in 1991, they were dismissed with scorn. The rule at FSU was not "Publish or perish," it was "Discuss or perish." And Spent was known to despise the "discussion method" of education. He was accused of "elitism" and of "harboring aggressive indifference to the values of postmodern modernity." Someone had told the committee that Spent had hysterical outbursts in the classroom, accusing students of "stomping civilization under the manure-clogged hooves of rock-and-roll bolshevism." On another occasion, it was reported, he had demanded that a student explain the function of "that polluted cyst growing on your shoulders that you are presumptuous enough to call a brain."

It should have come as no surprise to Spent. Some years earlier a man named Esau Bloomhart had gotten into a similar jam, although he was already tenured. He had taken to arranging chairs in his classroom in classic row formation rather than in the progressive circular mode. He also insisted that students sit on their chairs rather than on the floor, which was deeply annoying to the FSU establishment. It continued to be believed in the nineties, as it had been in the sixties, that the closer a person got to the ground, the wiser or the more beatified he became, which accounted, it was said, for the wisdom of boy-scout leaders and poverty-stricken gurus living out lives of resolute inaction in the gutters of old Delhi. Then Bloomhart was caught raging at knots of students sleeping nude in the hallway of the student union. Finally, in a sustained act of bitterness, he flunked six students in as many semesters. An indignant band of students petitioned for his dismissal. The petition went to the FSU Board of Peers, the top faculty governance body of the FSU teacher's union. The union was run by a no-nonsense, former longshoreman who was an adjunct professor of applied ethics in Spent's own department.

Bloomhart was given an option. He could resign, or he could be kicked out. He was reminded that records of the Board of Peers hearings would be sent to any other university he tried to work for and that a simple telephone call from the union boss would torpedo any attempt to outflank the Board of Peers. Bloomhart resigned and took his place in one of the breadlines on South Wabash Avenue.

Spent, however, had something going for him that Bloomhart did not. He was untenured, which meant that he taught three times as much as senior faculty did and was at their beck and call for grunt work. Day in and day out, his resentment buried deep within him, he trundled their heavy audio-visual equipment from classroom to classroom. A-V equipment was the core of FSU's educational delivery system and it was a rare day for Spent when he didn't make ten or twelve setups for senior instructors.

Faculty came to respect the grunt in Spent and they put up with his occasional tantrums about quality with the same tolerant and forgiving attitude that a mule driver displays toward an exceptionally strong but obstreperous animal. A certain bond of kindness and even friendship grew up between Spent and several of the senior faculty. Twice, in fact, when Spent, in print, had called FSU an intellectual cathouse, they rallied to save him from summary dismissal by Dean Puffit.

Through it all, FSU continued to thrive. It enrolled students by the tens of thousands, spewing them out each spring like fry from a fish hatchery. As far as Spent was concerned, they were a malignant rabble set loose on a defenseless American citizenry. But to Puffit, they were the bloom of a life's work.

The students arrived on the FSU campus in crusty jeans and billboard T-shirts, some on beaten motorcycles, many in jalopies with rotted-out bodies, some by trucks of the People Mover System. They had all read FSU promotion literature, or had someone read it to them. It promised quick, practical degrees that did not require sitting around in overheated libraries or steamy lecture halls. They gathered during registration week in the Plaza of Inspirations, some on uppers, some on downers, but all excitedly committed to Puffit's plan to bring the progressive education revolution—the one that John Dewey had started in 1899 with the tiny volume, *The School and Society*—to final fruition. In that book Dewey had outlined his dream of American education. It was to be a gigantic populist wallow.

The vision of the school-as-wallow had fallen out of favor briefly in the early eighties. There had been "calls for excellence" then and the idea was talked about a lot. But it did not materialize. Conservatives in the government, like conservatives everywhere, were suspicious of anything that implied reading a lot of books. They refused to put up money for anything requiring unnecessary learning. The liberals, on the other hand, shared the distrust of liberals everywhere for anything smacking of self-control. So anytime words like *discipline* popped up in the national debate on schools, they dragged their feet. Not much excellence was the result.

Puffit was the kind of man that thrived in a world that was not very sure of itself. Small, dark, compact, physically weak but seasoned-looking, his clothes tastefully chosen but democratic in implication, he knew what he wanted and usually got it. So when he took over the FSU School of Education he set out to make a name for himself. He built an entire new curriculum. It was to be popular in appeal, both cheap and plentiful. First he got rid of the concept of the past. He had little patience with anything or anybody that allowed the past more than a casual glance. The "hands-on practicum" was to be FSU's forte. A stream of new "Lifestyles" courses quickly came on line. There was "Wellness Lifestyles for Tomorrow," "Lifestyles for the Undermotivated," and even "Advanced Lifestyles in Having an Experience." The advanced course in "Having an Experience" was built on Dewey's renowned essay on that topic. (Puffit's job was made easier by the fact that the great philosopher had never said what it was like not to have an experience.)

In 1991, Puffit went all out in running down grants to support the new curriculum. He received a $20 million grant to support a scholarship program, funded through the Washington Office of Urban Societal Target Impact Task Force programs. OUSTIF, as the office was known, was established in 1988 and pushed hard for a nationwide system of "Lifestyle Betterment Scholarships." Puffit's school was so far ahead of the rest that he was able to corner two-thirds of the money available for the LBS awards.

Puffit kept qualification requirements for Lifestyles Betterment Scholarships simple but tough. To demonstrate their appreciation for the famed progressive maxim that the only thing unchanging was change itself, scholarship applicants could do one of two things. They could repeat from memory, without notes of any kind, lyrics from a best-selling rock composition, or, also from memory and without the help of notes or cribs, compression ratios of two Japanese motorcycle engines manufactured since 1988. Compression data taken from American snowmobiles was considered historical in nature, hence unacceptable.

The reason for tough entrance requirements, Puffit made clear, was that they were the only way the quality of the program could be assured and FSU's standards held above question. And to prevent students who got LBSs from forming a snobbish little elite on campus, the dean also established a back-up aid system known as the Office of Hands-On Aid. It disbursed twenty-dollar bills each Tuesday morning at the Student Union.

Puffit put a tough young female student in charge of the Hands-On Aid Office. She was something of a campus celebrity when he found her, a rising star in a new musical form called puke rock. Puke rock was a post–punk rock sensation of the nineties. It got its name from the uninhibited vomiting that had become de rigueur for doped-up concert audiences.

The puke rock star that Puffit hand-picked for the tough new administrative assignment had become especially adept at small, discrete, on-stage ejaculations of vomit between refrains of puke rock classics. She came to the FSU campus on Tuesdays and Thursdays to undergo syphilis therapy at the student clinic and to attend Lifestyle classes. Each Tuesday morning, sitting on a stool behind the Hands-On disbursement window, she put students through their paces with questions that went to the heart of the era in which Chicago's young people moved and breathed and had their being. "What is the current best-selling puke rock record?" "Why is it about the weather?" "Who got the

Emmy last month for the documentary on ulcers of the rectum in gays?" "Do you think the weather is the reason why the sixty-nine ain't seen on television no more?"

The young lady was an imposing figure. Her head was shaved in front and at the rear a snarl of hair coiffed to resemble the rump of a Labrador retriever hung to her shoulders. Her face was painted in vivid stripes, mostly purple on one side, mostly British hunting green on the other. A small, rusted safety pin which caused the flesh to suppurate slightly where it entered and exited from the skin, delicately punctured her left cheek. Because of her gentle but firm manner at the Hands-On window, many students considered her a saint. Puffit shared that view, but for his own ulterior reasons. He wanted to give Washington the impression that he ran a tight ship. The young lady's rigorous enforcement of Puffit's hard line toward freeloaders meant that FSU seldom disbursed more than three hundred twenty-dollar bills a week at the Hands-On window.

In the past, FSU students had occasionally rebelled against tight regulation of their lives by people such as the Hands-On administrator. In 1991 they went on strike against formal commencement exercises. "NO MORE MOTHER FUCKIN' EXHORTATIONS" was scrawled on the reformers' placards. A NMMFE organization quickly sprang up and flourished.

Anselm Pester, professor and chairperson of Spent's own department of Urban Lifestyles Reconstructionist Philosophy, led the strike against commencement exercises. He took a leaf from Gandhi and went on his own kind of hunger strike. During the mass demonstrations in front of the chancellor's office, during which FSU students fried their brains with every drug they could get their hands on, Pester calmly refused to use anything but herbicide-contaminated marijuana. He would keep it up, he announced to the press, until university administration got its head straight and called off their stupefying commencement speeches. It was a popular cause, and fearing the bad press that would result if Pester died on the spot from scalded lungs, the administration acceded.

So Pester became something of a folk hero on campus. His reputation now reached far beyond his renown as a bulwark in the Lifestyles curriculum and recipient of the FSU Futurist Lifestyles Award. It went beyond his growing fame as a resolute switch-hitter and student of the works of de Sade and Hefner as well as lesser role models from the world of pedophilia. He was, he said, in the business of institution building and he would interface, he said, with any idea or anybody that served that end. And he often did.

So the commencement exercises ended despite grievous damage to the oratorical futures of campus deans and the chancellor. Thereafter the university sent out its diplomas by mail, tens of thousands of them, fourth class. The procedure was, Puffit boasted, as close to antielitism as university administrators could make it.

All of this took place against the singular story of FSU's rise to prominence. And by 1997, when the greenhouse effect began to make Chicago as hot in the winter as Mombasa was in the summer, stories of those early crisis years had begun to jell into the stuff of legend. Stories about the commencement exercises revolt were told and retold again and again. Stories about Chicago's great gangster era slowly got woven into the stories about FSU. It was tradition in the making. Clusters of torpid students lying about in their underwear in the shade of the great concrete high-rises that stood at the corners of the Plaza of Inspirations repeated the stories endlessly. And faculty, trading on the fact that Freedom State was almost ten years old, began to call it "Old FSU." Repugnant as the idea was to Tom Puffit, the university was putting down roots, settling in, generating a history and being captured by it.

As Spent and Puffit settled in at their table at Cirroco's Puffit ordered manhattans, his on the rocks in a tub, Spent's straight up. He didn't wait for the drinks to arrive before getting to the point.

"What do you think of the burglary of my office last week?" he asked. "Do you think the thing was an inside job?"

Spent knew Puffit loved contact sports, and he could recognize a power play when he saw one.

"I heard. Of course I think it was an inside job. Fact is, I'm certain of it."

Puffit was not above gang tackling. "Certain? None of the other faculty thinks it was. The police don't think so. I don't think so." His eyes were narrow. He sipped the drink placed before him. "Philosophy is one thing, burglary is another."

"To the layman. Only to the layman," Spent said, twisting for a few more yards. "But the evidence is all there."

"Where?" There was challenge in Puffit's voice.

Spent ticked off the highlights for extra yardage. He noted that the outside door of the building was left open. He noted that the dean's door had been locked, and that it was undamaged. He twisted into the end zone. "The transom above your door was open, Tom," he said with a small grin.

"So?" Puffit asked with a touch of aggression, challenging the score. "How in hell could they get through that transom? It's too damn small for a body to squeeze through."

It was time, Spent said to himself, to stop playing games. "Simple," he said firmly. "One of the gang was a pygmy or a . . . ?" He let the question hang. Fill in the blank, smart-ass, he thought.

Puffit cleared his throat. He was stumped.

Spent finished the thought for him. "Or? A midget!"

Puffit took another sip of his drink, a long, impatient sip, a real swig, in fact, Spent thought.

"It's all quite obvious, Tom, really," said Spent. "Pygmies are rare in our part of the world. Midgets are fairly common. Midgets are exceptionally curious organisms . . . because of the visual deprivation they experience living close to the ground. They take to this sort of thing." He paused. "Ergo?"

Puffit hung back. He was not sure what Spent was aiming at. The fact was that the dean kept a hefty supply of dope in his office. It could have been the target of the break-in. His supply ran the gamut, from reds to yellows and back again, coke, pot, snow, even old-fashioned Valium. Sometimes, with the office door locked, when an adventurous feeling came over him, he would take a quick little toboggan trip, toss a little of each into the hopper, then, depending upon which of the crafty little molecules chanced to invade this or that synapse first, flip out, snooze in his big office chair or do odd little belly flops on the shag rug, his elbows in, his legs spread, in a movement once observed in grounded Arctic seals.

Some weeks before their lunch Puffit had talked Jenny Perch into sharing one of his toboggan trips. He had fancied them together on the rug doing those belly flops. He assumed they would make her passionate. But she only turned deathly white, passed out briefly and ended up with a violent headache and ringing ears. Puffit's plan to take advantage of her if she passed out failed miserably. At the height of his opportunity he collapsed in his large executive chair and then slid, unconscious and twitching, under his desk, banging his head mercilessly on the underside of the front drawer in the process.

"The police should round up all the midgets in the city and cull them," Spent said, his tone nonchalant.

"Cull them?" the dean asked, his eyebrows well above where they belonged.

"Right. I have already calculated a 'transom unit measure,' Tom. For just that purpose. It's a classic exercise in taxonomy."

Spent outlined the essentials of TUM. It was really an elementary principle, he explained, in concept at least. One calculated the narrowest dimension of the transom through which burglars are suspected of entering a room. Normally this is the height of the transom, which can run up to a foot and a half. Breadths are normally broader, up to three feet and a half. Cross-sectional calculations are then computed for the suspects. TUM immediately separates the potentially guilty from the innocent. Large and rotund suspects, for instance, can be assumed innocent. They can be allowed to return to normal life as responsible members of the community. He added that special caution must be taken, of course, with large or rotund suspects known to have studied yoga.

The dean tore off a piece of sesame bun, buttered it, nibbled at it, then put it down. He brushed the seeds around his plate into a pile, arranging them into a small pyramid with his knife, then scattered them with a snap of his little finger. After stammering an indistinct reference to the "remarkable individuality in each of us," he ordered another round of drinks. "Have you talked with anyone else about your 'transom unit measure'?"

Puffit hoped Spent had. It would be the straw that broke the camel's back, exactly what he needed to prove that Spent was plain damn nuts. He could fire the arrogant bastard then and there, have done with it.

When Spent said he hadn't told a soul and that the transom unit measure was the kind of idea one didn't just bandy about, its potential being what it was, Puffit grumbled, "Too bad. Too bad. Now let's eat."

They ordered their food, Puffit selecting Scampi Cirroco, the house luncheon specialty. Spent chose a casserole with tripe. As they sipped their manhattans Puffit winked at Spent over the rim of his cocktail tub. "We are what we eat, you know."

The crack about his tripe rankled Spent. He knew the name of that game. It was all very psychiatric. Reaction formation, that old screwed if you do, screwed if you don't caper. Tripe is an understated dish; hence enjoyment of it betrayed evidence of self-doubt, compensation, a form of cover-up, fright turned inside out. In a word, arrogance. Spent's face twisted in a small, half-moon-shaped smile. "Eating animal entrails the mark of an obsequious carnivore, Tom?" he asked.

Puffit's face constricted. "I don't get it."

Spent was not about to allow Puffit to strangle him with an intestine. "Are you implying, dean, that tripe eaters are closet fascists, or merely passive-aggressive?"

The dean stammered. They were now playing chess, Spent realized, with a post-neo-Freudian twist. But Puffit was playing recklessly and Spent had nailed him with the closet fascist question; nailed him with a horse fork, a knight on both his king and queen.

Spent let the dean wiggle for a moment, then said, "Why should tripe be anything but the logical choice for me? On top of teaching I have to counsel the malignant rabble in our school. Counselors are the cloaca of a university. It all goes through them."

"Cloaca?" Puffit frowned. "Not sure I'm familiar with the term."

The half-moon turned the corner of Spent's mouth up

again. "It's a new generation of desk computer, Tom. Ask Hodgkiss about it. Purchasing agents know about things like that." He knew Puffit would. It would be checkmate in absentia, thought Spent, the kind from which big shots find it hard to recover.

Puffit sensed vaguely that Spent had booby-trapped him somehow, or tied a tin can to his leg, but he went for the initiative again. "Next year we'll have some new advanced courses in leadership lifestyle alternatives... including use of the pocket computer. And our new Lifestyles and UFO Design course will then come on line."

Puffit had abruptly turned Spent's flank, and Spent realized it. The Dean was obviously putting a lot of money on the future of the school's work in the UFO area. Realizing that the train was about to leave the station and he had best be on it, Spent said, "Sounds like you've come up with something, Tom."

"We have. That's for damned sure, Spent. Damned sure."

Spent immediately climbed aboard. "Why not call the new courses Traditions in UFO Design?"

Puffit did not like the reference to the past. He frowned. "As you know, professor, I personally am strongly opposed to the concept of the past. But I will admit that futurist traditions interest me. We might be able to mount such a program if faculty are willing to put in place a hands-on audio-visual learning mode as its delivery system. The college can use up-front money for the bottom line."

"That would help. I mean the hands-on A-V mode, bypass the problem of student illiteracy," Spent nodded.

"That whole literacy thing is a bogus problem, Spent," said Puffit. "A forgery."

"A forgery, Tom?" Spent was delighted at the prospect of another ambush.

Puffit stiffened in his chair. "Hell, in a postmodern world literacy is the opium of the learned classes." He fumbled with his tie, pulled it off impatiently and stuffed it into his pocket. "Never liked these sonsabitchin' middle-class nooses," he grumbled.

"Man is born free, but everywhere he ends up wearing a tie," Spent said, trying to be playful.

Puffit was not amused.

"A new curriculum built on UFO tradition could pull down a hefty grant," Spent soothed. "Some of the new people in Washington are looking for bright ideas. A good proposal would act like a magnet. The fact is it would act like a black hole in space, suck everything into it."

The black hole metaphor struck home. A seraphic smile spread across Puffit's face. But Spent knew a pride of authorship issue was about to surface. He, after all, had come with the idea of a proposal with black hole properties. But it was time for calm on both sides, he said to himself. He concentrated on the tripe placed before him.

Puffit chewed his food slowly and deliberately. "In today's high-tech world it's no longer necessary to put up with that literacy crap. To be sure, we will have to retain a number of scribes, men and women—and for that matter those who do not wish to choose either sex—to continue working with the written word, math, computers and what have you. But they'll be a servant class, Spent. We should never forget that."

Spent sensed that he had gained some ground and offered to buy drinks. Puffit nodded.

"Computer people are postmodern scribes, Casper," the dean went on. "They work to preserve the fruits of postmodernism. No different than the scribes of ancient Egypt. Except that in our world the fuckin' Pharaohs are gone, thank God."

"Thank Isis," said Spent.

Puffit looked bewildered for a moment. "What the hell has that got to do with what I'm saying?" Without waiting for Spent's answer, he continued. "The common person in America, Casper, the person next door, the person whose plow broke the plains, the same person celebrated in Copland's 'Fanfare for the Common Person' (the Dean had taken the liberty to adjust the title of the work) has finally been put in place."

"A throne room in every tenement apartment; a chicken in every pot," Spent said, adding what he thought would be a touch of levity.

But Puffit was annoyed. He squinted at Spent over his uplifted fork. "You can really be a reactionary shitface, you know that? An elitist prick."

"Guilty of high pride and misdemeanors, dean?"

Puffit ignored the question. "A free society cannot allow itself to be ensnared in the kind of traditionalism that hides behind all that shit about literacy. Everything is available in pictures now anyway. All the *best* magazines are pictures, with a dab of writing here and there, in computer printout form, of course. All the really *popular* magazines are pictures." He paused pensively, then sipped his drink. "And I'm not afraid of that word *postpop* either! What would this society be without postpop? Nothing! Not a goddamned thing, Spent. And pictures are part of it; damn near all of it... and printouts, of course."

"A lot of hands-on audio-visual material has been put in place," Spent said. "No doubt about it."

Puffit's thoughts rolled on. "Even the magazine *Genitals* has become entirely hands-on visual stuff. Three-D foldouts, everything. Brilliant use of the visual mode. Postmodern and post-McLuhan. Witty, clever, functional."

"Post-Warholian too, would you say, dean?"

But there was no stopping the dean's train of thought. It possessed the brute momentum of boldly reconstructed truth. "And where but in America could this whole revolutionary thing take place? It's awesome when you think about it. Whole cities crowded with men, women and altereds, coming and going daily, all futurists, not reading a damn thing, finally free, finally liberated." Puffit stared past Spent, his eyes clouded with emotion. "Back when I was a grad student in Columbia's College of Ed they said that some day we would come this far. And they were right. Right as rain."

"It's been a long journey, dean."

Puffit went on, biting his lip. "What the hell do people think those poor barefoot fuckers stood around in the snow at Valley Forge for, if not this? And all that slaughter at Gettysburg?"

"Amnesia, thou divine intoxicant..." Spent intoned.

"Well, whatever," said Puffit. "We can put the future up front where it belongs. It's the bottom line. The future! That's where I'm coming from."

"Nothing like the future to give a man a unique perspective, Tom," said Spent. He settled back to let the whole thing seep into Puffit, the future, the solution to the burglary, his proposal for an educational breakthrough, the idea of a whopping grant from the Department of Education.

"You've been working too hard lately," Puffit said, a shrimp skewered on his fork. "You seldom leave the office until late in the afternoon, I'm told. I have it too, Casper, that you're hitting the bottle in your office. Hitting it hard."

Spent was knocked off balance. "Just a bit now and then," he stammered, "to relax and clear my head."

The dean's eyes narrowed to impatient little slits. "We don't mind drinking, you know that! We're a forward-looking social reconstructionist institution. Of course, we'd prefer you switched to grass. Students would respect you more. But I'm troubled by something else. You've been dropping snobbish little remarks to the minority students. Like making reference to Chivas Regal to your black students, then snide little remarks when they ask if it has a V–8 engine. Cruel, tasteless remarks. And telling Chicano students who can't answer your questions that they are still 'wetbacks behind the ears.' I don't like it, Spent. Not a damned bit. And I'm ready to do something about it." Puffit looked to one side, then at the waiter. He signaled for the check with an impatient little circling gesture of the hand.

"You're going to pick up the tab, Tom?" Spent asked ingenuously.

The dean made a small snorting noise. "Spent," he said, a sullen look on his face, "the students say you refer to our university as Operation Sow's Ear. That correct?"

"Only relative to silk-purse goals."

Puffit snapped, "Goals are all right. We do not object to goals. In fact we have taken a leaf from the federal agencies. We now have both goals *and* objectives. But what about the student that came in to see me and told me—told me with considerable anxiety, Spent—that you told him, and I quote, 'Flee this backwater before you take on the smell of it.' That true?"

"Only to let the student know that he was good enough to go to the grad school at the University of Chicago."

"Exactly! Exactly!" Puffit was heating up again. He glared at Spent, then drank the ice water that lay in the bottom of his cocktail glass. "Have you ever looked at the brick wall those snobs at Chicago have built around their campus? Have you? Almost ten feet high, with barbed wire along the top, and checkpoints, for Christ's sake, on Drexel and over on Fifty-seventh. They cover their elitist crap by calling it the Robert Maynard Hutchins Wall. They say vandals won't let them do their goddamned research. They say they can't use their little chapel because people out there looking for a place to sleep piss all over the aisles. Who the hell are they kidding? And do they produce leaders? Hell, no. *Thinkers* is their line. Who in hell needs thinkers? Do you think this weather thing calls for thinkers? It calls for leaders! People willing to get things moving again. And FSU is out to make *leaders,* not thinkers. Any damn fool can think!" Then, as he throttled back, he added, "I think you ought to take a leave, beginning in October. I already talked to your department chair about it. Pester agrees."

"I don't have tenure, Tom, you know that," Spent said. "Leaves can be tricky for untenured faculty." He watched the dean's face. The dean, he was now convinced, was about to make a move on the transom unit measure idea. Trying to elbow up the bar for a free one on me, Spent told himself.

But of course Spent was wrong. Puffit had other goals, other objectives as well. "There's even suspicion that the break-in of my office had something to do with those grades," Puffit said. "Students trying to find out why we let you stay on at FSU."

Spent spooned the bottom of his empty bowl and kept his counsel.

"Certainly that burglary was an oddly hostile gesture considering my well-known stand on the legalization of crime," Puffit said. "I don't have to tell you that more than a little suspicion in all of this points at you."

Spent swallowed hard. He hadn't the remotest notion who had broken into Puffit's office. But suddenly fingers were pointing at him, or Puffit was arranging things that way. The invitation to lunch had not been a response to either the power or the pith of his memorandum. It was an invitation to mount the platform and accept the blade of the guillotine. He could feel the blade high above him there at lunch. With a wave of the hand Puffit could send it crashing. It would slice clean as a whistle through Spent's life, severing his dreams of what might have been. He tried to talk. He wanted to say something to the crowd, from high on that hideous platform, something that would sway the executioner, get the whole ridiculous thing called off. Only a mutter came out, and the mutter sounded impudent to Puffit. More of the same.

"I know where you're coming from, Spent, don't give me that. You peddled the same shit last year when you complained about students abusing teachers in the classroom. This is a *school of education,* and don't forget it. How in hell do you think we can prepare our teachers for the high schools if we don't expose them to student abuse here? Tell me! How?"

Puffit was flushed. He was furious now, and dangerous. "Shit," he went on, "you give me a pain in the ass. Don't you ever think of the kind of homes our students come from?"

Something unconquerable in Spent, perhaps the spirit of De Gaulle hovering near the table, resentful about that crack about his nose and Adam's apple said, "You mean the penitentiary, dean?"

Puffit glowered, his lips tight. "I know you, Spent. I know you. I heard about that speech you made to the minority students who asked you to drop those flunk grades. You ranted to them about the work ethic. You said, 'Slavery has proved an ineffective way to teach the work ethic!' How goddamned smug can a person get! Ever hear of robot technology? I got news for you. It's come on line. It's been put in place. That work-ethic bullshit is as obsolete as reading."

"Ora et labora," Spent said, his defiance giving him new strength. "The question is, when will robots learn to pray?"

Puffit turned cold and disdainful. "You got a problem, Spent. You're not too tightly wrapped. And you're an elitist. You're probably a fucking monarchist, if the truth were known."

"If the truth were known, dean, there would be no need for this conversation," said Spent, his chin high now, invincible, without fear.

"We don't need your kind at FSU." The blade came down.

A small, defiant remark came up from the basket. "I may be fired, dean, but I'm not dead."

Puffit seized the check, scanned it, put down a couple of bills and they left. As Spent parted with Puffit at the door, the dean's final comment was, "So you can knock off the whimpering. Being on relief for a while will teach you something about the work ethic."

CHAPTER 4

Three days after Spent was told he would not be rehired in the fall, he bumped into Delbert Dooley, the registrar at FSU. Dooley, too, was a member of the dogged little tribe that lived in the Indiana Dunes National Park area and continued to commute to Chicago on the old South Shore line after the collapse of the Fastram system. He was a man of average height, perhaps five feet ten, about a hundred and sixty-five pounds. He had a pleasant, open-looking face, with a youthful, somewhat freckled complexion and reddish hair. He had hit thirty-eight on his last birthday and had it not been for the harried look in his eyes one would have taken him for thirty or thirty-one. He had married a typist at FSU, and when Spent told him of the beauty of the dunes country they bought a house there, next door to where Spent lived with his sister Dorothy and brother-in-law Swag.

Dooley motioned Spent to take a seat next to him. "I heard about things at school, Cass," he said as Spent squeezed into the seat next to him.

"Heard about what?"

"That Puffit fired you."

"Taking a leave of absence, that's all."

"Way I heard it, the university's taking a leave from you."

As soon as he had made the remark, Dooley blushed. He liked Spent and knew that his playful poke at him had come off badly. "Sorry," he added apologetically. "That was a mean way to put it."

Spent was annoyed. "It becomes you, Del."

Dooley tried to patch things up. "I didn't mean it that way. I know what it's like to be down. I'm down now, in a way. Suffering from shingles again. It's a built-in hair shirt. Around the waist is worst. Itches like fury. Sometimes I can't go to the office. I just sit on the edge of the damn bed and scratch by the hour. Now this heat thing. It's killing me, Cass. I swear to God it is. And those peckers in Washington aren't doing a damn thing about it. They could shut down some of those plants around Pittsburgh and here in Gary, let the air clear up. They say we can't cut back any further. I don't believe them. Or they could have demanded those scrubbers on the stacks."

Spent said, "The cause of your shingles is a virus, herpes zoster, as distinguished from herpes simplex, herpes gestationis and herpes tonsurans. Enters the nerve bundle on the sly."

"I can tell you one thing, they look like hell," said Dooley. "The skin around my waist reminds me of the bark of a burr oak."

"Look at it this way, Del. You're really fortunate."

"Fortunate? For getting shingles? That's a new one."

"Fortunate ontologically, Del. Scratching is proof of existence. As Descartes might put it, 'I itch, therefore I am.' You have the foundation for a philosophy of the self. The itch in most men is too vague to serve as foundation for anything, except infidelity perhaps."

Dooley wiped the sweat from his head, then slumped in his seat and closed his eyes. "Lay off, for Christ's sake, Cass. I'm sorry I was snooty about you getting the sack." Dooley was bewildered by Spent, as most people were. He was never sure whether Spent was being serious or not. Now it was his ontological proof of existence. The man was a nut, likable enough, but a nut nevertheless, and like most nuts hard to get really close to. Dooley was never sure if the gate was open, closed or simply loose on a hinge. "Oh, God," he said finally and seemed to drop off to sleep.

Spent sat upright in the seat, listening to the rattle of the coach. He studied the ancient wainscoting on the ceiling. Here and there its original golden brown varnish shone through the sloppy coat of aluminum paint that was intended to give the coaches an up-to-date look, more acceptable to riders used to the high-tech luxury of the Fastram system.

Fastram trains had whizzed along at 190 miles an hour and broke for stops with the soft ease of a womanly caress. Its coaches were richly appointed, each car with a different theme, one from the Gay Nineties, another from the Roaring Twenties, one with eighteenth-century French accoutrements, one done up as if it were a grimy lavatory pickup spot in San Francisco, another in Pompeiian villa style, and several with space-age planetary murals and glittering chrome-trimmed, cast-plastic seats. In the club car, martinis and scotch flowed in buckets, at permanent happy-hour prices. The latest puke rock musical treasures were piped in from a disc-jockey-operated studio in a front car directly behind the train's mighty cryogenically cooled super turbos. And in the last car, labeled "The Flick Fashion Caboose," the latest wrinkle in sexual fashion was touted on an eight-foot-square screen. Many shows were beamed live by satellite from pornographic motion picture studios unaccountably thriving in Luxembourg. Some attributed the Luxembourg renaissance to leftovers of Arab oil money. Others merely said that the little duchy was finally getting with it.

Spent had always felt uneasy in the Flick Fashion Caboose and he usually hung out in the club car. The new hedonism baffled him. In fact, postmodern debauchery left him bewildered. Sadomasochism gave him chills, especially when children were the subject, which made him wonder at times if his detractors weren't correct when they said he was hopelessly out of step with his times. It was this reaction to life on the Fastram that generated his love-hate feeling for the old South Shore train.

The sound of the old trains often cast a spell over him. He could hear the wheels, "I-told-you-so, I-told-you-so, I-told-you-so," mile after mile. And even though he had a difficult time cramming his long body, almost six feet three inches of it, into the old seats, and his joints and muscles ached, went through spasms and grew numb in places, he took a kind of perverse delight in seeking out car number 431, just to watch the huge greenish stain creep across the ceiling of the old coach. Train management had apparently tried to seal the leaking roof with blacktop sealer, purchased jointly with the highway department as an economy measure.

He was feeling quite smug about the whole thing when a palsied old woman, her hands quivering, her head jerking about in tiny, rhythmic tremors, got on the train at the Roosevelt Road stop and stood clutching the handle on the back of the seat two rows ahead of where Spent and Dooley sat.

A shouting match suddenly erupted between her and a young woman sitting in the aisle seat next to where she stood. The young woman, her hair clipped short and brushed forward in a tight little helmet, the fashionable mental patient cut persisting from the eighties, ripped into the palsied old woman. "Stare at me with that shitface as much as you want. I ain't givin' up this seat," she shouted. "I got here first."

The old woman, her voice high, cackling but unintimidated, yelled back that it was more than the weather that was wrong in America. "It's all you young ones. You just don't care about anything but yourselves." Her deep, watery gray eyes took on the fierce look of an animal at bay.

"It was you old farts that built all them fancy machines that don't work no more," the girl shouted. "You built that big, bloated Buick Electra rottin' in my backyard. So up yours, baby." She turned to the man across the aisle and asked, "Ain't that right, mister?"

He, a gentleman in his fifties, apparently a banker or a beleaguered executive, sweating it out in a soggy seersucker suit, looked sheepishly about, then got up and let the old lady have his seat.

"One born every minute," the young lady said loudly, turning toward the rear as if talking to Spent.

No reply was needed. At Hammond the train's wheels screeched and the car shuddered to a stop. Dooley banged forward in his seat and came awake. He mumbled, "Kay? That you?" Then he slid back into his dreams. Kay was his wife. Five months earlier she had left him and moved in with Anselm Pester.

"Easy does it, Del," said Spent. He took out his note pad and made one of the small drawings he used to illustrate his journals.

At Gary the train growled threateningly, came to a stop, moved forward a few yards, quivered and jolted to a stop. Several cars were uncoupled. The shock sent Dooley skidding forward across the wicker seat. He came up sharply, his rump on the floor.

"Good grief, Kay!" Dooley cried. "Must you be so violent?" His eyes widened as he looked up at Spent. "Cass, for God's sake, help me up from here."

Spent and another passenger dislodged Dooley and set him back on his seat. A betrayed look survived on Dooley's face behind the flush of embarrassment. He said, "Dreaming, I guess." Perspiration beaded his forehead.

"You all right?" Spent asked.

"My backbone took a hell of a scrape."

"Takes a lot of backbone to be a commuter these days."

"I'll live. Whether I can survive your jokes is another question," Dooley said.

"You'll survive, Del."

"I know what happened with Puffit and Pester," Dooley said, turning to Spent. "I know how you feel. I took it on the chin a few months ago too, you know. From that skunk Anselm Pester."

"You courted the calamity," Spent said without looking at Dooley.

"Kay was a lovely calamity."

"Well, you had to be trendy. You watched every love story that showed up on TV. That stuff got to her. That's why she demanded a career. Now she's got one, as a typist over in Purchasing. Instead of a nice warm dinner waiting for you at home, and a nice home furnished with that elegant knock-kneed Queen Anne furniture, and a baby Dooley playing on a fuzzy polyester rug, you end up with a woman who wears her sunglasses on top of her head and demands the right to sleep with anyone she wants, including Pester. Very now, Del. You into puke rock too?"

"If I ever catch up with that sonofabitch, I'll kill him. I'll..." Dooley could not finish.

"Venereal is chic, Del. Better get used to it."

"Those dirty limericks he collected? He had a pack of

three-by-five cards typed up, one on each card. Kay typed it all during working hours. That's two hundred and twenty-five cards. I calculated it."

"Awesome achievement in its way, Del. Monumental, both in form and content. Some day it will stand alongside Baudelaire."

Dooley looked at Spent. "Here we go again." Then his mind slipped back into thoughts of his wife. "God, how I love that woman," he said. He stared out the window of the train.

Spent remembered seeing Pester and Kay in the cafeteria often, after she had left Dooley. They would sit at one of the tables near the plastic fork-and-knife dispenser, tirelessly culling the card index for some misplaced rhyme. They sat there for hours, sweating like blacksmiths in hell, hammering one line after another into form, giggling, quivering, transported. "Oh, they're so spicy!" she would squeal. "And a real form of artistic discipline too. That's the anapestic form. Composing in five anapestic lines isn't easy."

How she loved the word *anapestic.* So Pester promptly worked it into a limerick about a fat Italian wife who became spastic with passion whenever she fed her dog. And then he composed a special limerick for her birthday, about odd-shaped and persevering penises, proud and self-righteous as Pharisees at prayer. The beauty of it all swamped the girl's mind. She was under his spell for good.

Dooley turned toward Spent. "He knew how to get a woman, Cass. First that philosophy crap. 'A philosophy for our free and wonderfully shipwrecked age.' He pumped her full of that during coffee breaks at school. She told me all about it before she left. She said it was fate. 'I'm doomed by fate to love him,' she said. She wept and had temper tantrums like you can't imagine. They snorted cocaine. She said she felt so happy when she did that she wanted to kill herself." He leaned back in his seat and closed his eyes again.

Spent watched the landscape roll by. The rows of huge warehouses east of Gary were mostly empty, their huge two-story doors pushed back. A pair of stray dogs chased one another in and out of a small run-down, doorless guardhouse near the largest of them. A forest of electric power line towers appeared, their limp, high voltage lines still lethal with power being delivered to factories along the lake to the north. Then tank farms by the mile, huge discus shapes, patched and peeling. Several had collapsed during a fire a year ago and lay melted in strange black Dali forms.

Near Burns Ditch, several bulldozers were busy working overtime, with high power headlights illuminating the evening gloom. They were filling in a small patch of wetland that had somehow escaped the notice of industrialists a year ago. They grunted and shoved back and forth, burying swaying bullrushes and cattails under a slag of clay and festering rubbish trucked in from Chicago. To fend off environmentalists, a few of whom still lived like angry hermits out around the Dunes National Park, they had put up a large, nicely lettered sign in red, white and blue. "We want jobs, not picnic grounds!" It was signed "Local 416, Demolition Workers for a Better Tomorrow."

At Burns Ditch, clouds of heavy smoke and soot skulked about the stacks of two great steel mills recently completed in Kempt's reindustrialization drive. They were largely automated, but without expensive smog precipitators on the stacks. They would help put the Japanese back in their place, Kempt had announced, especially Shingu and Roanji corporations, both of which had managed, by some miracle of effort and imagination, to move their steel plants out of the flooded lowlands near Osaka into hills near Kyoto.

Spent watched the huge, dirty gray clouds turn slowly in the wind coming off the lake. Great evil-looking faces formed in the smoke, then dissolved and formed again.

"I got a card from Kay yesterday," Dooley said suddenly without opening his eyes. "Look, it's a limerick about the mating habits of fleas." He reached into his coat pocket for the card and gave it to Spent.

"So it is," Spent said, genuinely surprised. "An anapestic affront."

"Do you think they're laughing behind my back?"

"All laughter takes place behind someone's back, Del. The shape of the planet makes that certain."

"You're right, of course. Just never thought of it that way."

"As for fleas, any of the order of Siphonaptera possess the most complex sex parts known. Their copulation is a deed of both skill and daring. You can check it out in the nineteen eighty report on the first International Conference on Fleas. Sir Vincent Wigglesworth made the opening address." Spent arched an eyebrow proudly.

"Makes a person wish he was a flea, I suppose," Dooley said, chuckling.

"It's an evolutionary mandate, Del. But I am not convinced that insects will inherit the earth after this greenhouse thing kills off all the humans. Don't wager your reputation on the insect. Most are poltroons when put to the test. Consider the snout beetle. It has three parts of its jaw combined into a drill. It uses this absurd tool to bore holes in acorns. Then it turns around and boorishly lays an egg in the hole. When the grub hatches, it lies about inside the acorn, in the dark where it's safe, gorging itself. Living dangerously? Nietzschean? Hardly! The contempt of the woodpecker is entirely understandable. But let us consider the snout beetle in greater detail..."

"Mind if we don't, Cass?" Spent's rattling on was getting to him.

"If you're not ready."

"I'm going to sue Pester for every penny he's got."

"That's not much, Del."

"I sold everything to do it, Cass, even my furniture. Saved the bed and one chair. That's why I never have anyone in. No place to sit."

Spent suddenly realized why Dooley kept his window shades down and had no one in for a beer, or even a Coke, for months. "We can always sit on the porch steps, Del."

"Pester should be arrested for peddling that filthy porno in class. I'm no prude, but some of that stuff is really degenerate. Like the junk he got hold of when that publishing house that just merged with the breakfast food company, Golden Toasties or some damn thing, came out with the memories of that Nazi bitch Ilse Köch. Pester and Kay made money on that crap. Charged kids a dollar to rent one of those booklets. They used the money to go to Canada to race greyhounds at one of those fancy new places on Hudson Bay."

Dooley sighed heavily. "I'm really tired tonight, Cass. Tired. Seems hotter than usual. But the weather people say it isn't. They say things are settling down. Puffit told me a plane spotted some ice near the North Pole just last week, a sheet almost a hundred miles long. His Commission on Public Information is going to broadcast pictures on TV."

Dooley pulled a battered album of family photographs from his briefcase and set it on his knees. They leafed through it, pages and pages of grinning relatives, including pictures of Kay as a baby, pop-eyed beneath a lace bonnet, garroted like a toy balloon. Dooley's eyes moistened.

Spent said, "Del, grief can only be subdued by will.

Emotion can be blunted only after it has been formed in patterns, sorted and cued. To avoid pain we must welcome unacceptable emotions, then arrange them in rectangles and pile them in cubes. Thereupon they assume the harmless symmetry of reflection."

Dooley looked out the window, then dabbed an eye. "Please, Cass," he said, trying to be gentle.

"Del," Spent said, "the first thing we must do is inventory the objects of your will. Would you mind ticking off those sensations that come..."

Dooley touched Spent's arm. "Please, Cass. Not now. I'm not in the mood for an inventory."

Spent did not let up. "Del, I quote the indomitable Dane, Kierkegaard, the magnificent humpbacked guardian at the gates to saintly insanity. 'Life can be understood backward, but it must be *lived* forward!'"

Dooley looked puzzled, then said, "Our wedding night was so wonderful...the stars were as big as street lights, the air as soft as crushed nylon."

Dooley closed the album.

"Good," said Spent, "turning the pages of old picture albums is a needless visit to a graveyard, and I might add that living in that house with the shades pulled down night and day is descending to the level of a centipede."

"I suppose so," said Dooley, finally giving in.

As they got off the train and waited on the siding for it to move on toward Beverly Shores, Spent suggested they stop at Kunst's tavern. "A couple of jolts will do us both good, Del."

Dooley said, "No. I'm not much of a drinker. Too old-fashioned."

"Old-fashioneds will go down just fine, Del," said Spent, misunderstanding.

"No. You just go home and sit down to one of your sister Dorothy's lovely dinners."

Wieners and beans? Spent thought. He was suddenly depressed.

Later in the evening, after the wieners and beans, Spent was sitting in his big gold lounge chair in his bedroom, unwinding with a few ad hoc CCs and water. He saw Dooley carrying a coil of rope and a massive iron hook into his house. Spent could not contain his curiosity. He walked over to where Dooley was fiddling about in his small flower garden, tying up snapdragons. Spent asked him what the big hook was for, and all that rope.

"Oh, nothing," Dooley said, his back to Spent. "Snapdragons in February. Nice, huh?"

The hook was almost two feet long. Spent was not put off. "What do you take me for, Del? Anybody of average intelligence knows what hooks are for."

Dooley drew himself up slowly, exasperation on his face. "Hooks have many purposes, Cass," he said. But he knew better than to let Spent crank up again. He knew he had had a few, so he pointed to some small cacti blooming yellow in the garden. "Lovely, aren't they? Moved them from the dunes. In the old days nobody would believe we had cactus in the dunes park." He moved toward the house to turn on the garden hose.

"Yes, they do seem suddenly right for Indiana," said Spent. Then he walked back to his own house and sat shirtless in his room in the big gold chair. He tossed off a reassuring CC and water.

CHAPTER 5

Dennis Swagmacher, or "Swag" as he was known locally, and his wife Dorothy had lived in the dunes area for over ten years. They moved there when Swag's mother, a great obese lady weighing almost three hundred pounds, died suddenly of bowel obstruction after an overly ardent encounter with one of her own masterpieces, prune dumplings with sauerkraut. Swag and Dorothy loved the woman deeply and when her house near Chesteron was vacated they took it as their duty not to sell it but to move in. The decision was made easier by the fact that Swag was out of work again. In fact, the automobile plant in Racine where he had been a sweeper had closed down for good. The plant's management said the factory was obsolete. And the public evidently felt the same way about the company's product.

Swag and Dorothy and their two little boys, Timmy and Kenny, fell in love with life in northern Indiana. Swag took odd jobs now and then, unemployment compensation and some public assistance when he could. Soon life was moving along in happy fits and starts as the Swagmachers made friends among the unemployed steel workers who had settled into the row of house trailers at the end of Waverly Road, near one of the park's swarming beaches. Swag's charm, in fact, was soon legendary in the area. He seemed to be liked by everyone. He quickly counted among his best friends every self-trained auto mechanic within ten miles, handy men of every sort, including a big rough-talking artist who lived in an old garage near Michigan City, and most bartenders within a fifteen-mile radius.

When Spent got up the morning of August third, he decided to take the 5:45 train into Chicago and eat at the cafe in the terminal under the Prudential Building. He could not face his sister wobbling about the kitchen in her saggy, lemon-colored housecoat, her hair a mousy snarl, mooning over the doggerel she found in the old Christmas cards she hoarded. Nor could he bear to watch Swag sitting in the kitchen in his undershirt, scratching his belly as he slurped his coffee. Their flirting and tickling alone was enough to drive him nuts.

The Koffee Klatch had, in the old air-conditioned days, a reputation as a pleasant little island, walled off by glass within the swirling throng of the terminal. With the heat it had turned into a hissing caldron, a hive of fractious fire ants who took turns sinking their mandibles into the rumps, cheeks, ankles and necks of their fellow man. Customers were snapping at waitresses, waitresses were snarling at busboys, busboys were biting their lips as they muttered nihilistic epithets.

A stool near where Spent was standing suddenly opened up. He slipped onto it. A pair of bloodshot eyes in the nearest agitated knot of fire ants skewered him. They belonged to a tall black girl. Her body was encased in a halter, tight blue jeans and white plastic boots with four-inch heels. "*Some* people will never understand what equal opportunity's all about," she said, mopping her forehead with the bright red kerchief tied about her neck.

Spent ordered a waffle and coffee. The waitress said, "Shit, man, we run outta batter. Be fifteen minutes 'fore a new batch is ready." He said he would have coffee while he waited. "Suit yourself," she said as she drew the coffee from the giant urn and skidded the cup to him across the counter.

Spent sipped and listened to the fire ants. Here and there about the room, above the din, came the toothy click of insult and counterinsult. The customer next to Spent joined in the distemper. He complained to the waitress of a sticky pancake-syrup bottle. She gave the bottle a quick wipe with a sour-smelling rag. "God! This is some life," she growled.

"One must be philosophic," Spent said.

"Yes, I guess so," she said. "But this is a real crock. And for livin' through this bullshit a person gets to die."

Spent was touched by her existential insight. It triggered an inspiration in him. He would, he thought to himself, alleviate some of the misery of such poor souls. "The proper design of syrup bottles would end the stickiness," he said.

The girl sighed. "Gimme a break, okay? No heavy thinkin' at this hour of the day."

"A few modest changes in design is all..."

"Your name Edison?"

"No. My name's Spent."

"Ain't surprised. Don't sound like you got much cash in your register."

"Not sure I follow you."

"Don't try. You been short-changed."

"I assure you, young lady, liquidity is not one of my problems."

"Well, you got trouble with a cracked container."

Spent absorbed the apparent discourtesy with a noncommittal nod. The inspiration was much too valuable to waste on a testy menial. He calmly drew out his pen and captured it on a napkin. The idea was simple enough. It would involve three bypass tubes running back into the bottle from a circular drain collar set below the spigot, thus preventing both dripping *and* costly waste. The outer convolutions imposed by the bypass would merely assure a better grip, safer handling and less syrup in the lap. And decorative decals would transform an otherwise rude and common object into a charming objet d'art. A decal reading "Fide et Fortitude" seemed about right. He folded the napkin and put it in his jacket for safekeeping. Patent procedures could come later.

Spent waited for a report on the batter. Nothing. Then a prim gentleman, one of the urban-planning faculty at FSU, came in. He was dressed in a seersucker jacket with red piping on the lapels, and, of course, a paisley ascot. He carried an umbrella. (It had not rained in months.) He sat down next to Spent and ordered prunes, toast and coffee. When the prunes arrived, he stared at them for a long moment, then poked them squeamishly with his spoon as if they might be alive. He called the waitress over and complained of their "squishy" texture. The head waitress was in the vicinity and overheard the remark. She strode over, leaned on the counter in front of him, pushed her great caribou face into his and said, "Eat your fruit, fruit!"

The man was affronted. He rose slowly, stood tall, tugged at his ascot and demanded the girl's name and that of her supervisor. He said her remarks were "tantamount to libel."

"Buster, when you dress the way you do, you ain't libeled nobody but yourself," she said as she picked up the dirty plates and silver from the counter next to him.

He was unequal to the firmness of her blow. He grumbled something about bigotry and genetics and walked out.

The caribou turned to the waitress serving Spent and sneered, "Get that, sweetheart. He claims he's got genetics. I wonder where he hangs 'em?"

But still no waffle. Spent caught the attention of his waitress as she moved to serve another customer, and told her he would have a Danish and more coffee. She said they were out of Danish. He asked what he might have instead.

"Warm apricots," she said. He asked what else she might have.

"I got lots of everything but time, so make up your mind." He settled for the apricots. As she dumped them in front of him and refilled his coffee cup she winked at the caribou. The caribou grinned at her and said, just loud enough for Spent to hear, "Here's another one to make your day. With a beak like that I bet he eats the seeds first."

Spent had had enough. He pushed the apricots back slowly, demanded the check and went to the cashier to pay. He told the cashier that their coffee tasted like the Chicago River smelled. But the fool in the fire ant prevailed. She took it as a compliment. "Oh, thank you. Thank you. We do use specially softened water, you know." He suppressed a scream as he pushed through the door. He would have a nip in the office to set things right.

But that, too, took on its special complication. He met Anselm Pester in the hall in front of his office door. "Just checking things out," said Pester.

"Right, Anselm," said Spent. "What else would our esteemed department chairman be doing with a passkey stuck in my office door?"

"Your window's broken, Casper. Secretary noticed the sound. Windy as hell out today. You know I wouldn't..."

"I know you wouldn't..."

Pester was in his threadbare jeans with a cotton shirt loose at the waist. It was evidently made in Guatemala. A giant quetzal bird swept across his chest and buried its beak somewhere near his belt buckle. Noting Pester's hairless head bulging up through a Marxist-Leninist beard, Spent could not resist asking, "Out to pick some coffee beans, Anselm?"

Pester pretended to ignore Spent as he fought to retrieve his key. Over his shoulder he said, "And what has Professor Spent been doing lately besides dicing criminals?"

It was clear to Spent that Puffit had been talking about the transom unit measure. But it was more than that. It was an opening move in the little chess game Pester and Spent played during their brief hallway encounters. It was an impudent question, typical of Spent's style, pawn to king's four, as the chess manuals would put it.

Spent answered by sliding to one side of the issue, pushing his own pawn to the king's row. "I spend most of each day studying the billowing lunacy of faculty at old FSU." (Pawn to king's four.)

"Then you are no doubt interested in hypervolumes. I have just published a paper on the bloating of capitalists. I've placed it in the *Journal of Materialist Erotic Perceptions*. You may have heard of the journal. It's published in San Francisco. Unisex Press." (Gutsy move, knight to queen's bishop's three.)

"Oh, of course. I read that journal as if it were going out of style." (Knight up front to the queen's bishop's three. A solid move.)

"Hrrumpff." (A flustered move, bishop to knight's five.)

"Hypervolumes have always interested me," Spent said. "Mostly for what they imply for living on a planet that may be going flat. Poses real problems in navigation. Sailing off the edge of the earth can be an unsettling experience." (Knight to bishop's three.)

"You are right, of course. We accept Columbus' view of the planet merely because of scientific convention. (A cagey move, pawn to queen's three.)

"Because of the loss of nerve in postmodern man? Takes a lot more guts to sail a cube than it does to sail a ball." (An unpretentious move, pawn to the bishop's three.)

Pester answered with pawn to the king's knight's three. "And what would you recommend to deal with this loss of courage in postmodern man?"

"Inventiveness. Imagination!" Spent said firmly. "Gear that would permit us to negotiate our decline and fall. Not high tech, Anselm. Merely sails that turn into parachutes."

Pester frowned.

"I have made sketches of that very thing," Spent added casually.

Pester was nonplussed. He tried to take himself out of the game as he jiggled the key still stuck in Spent's office door. "This miserable sonofabitch!"

It was all over but the apologizing, thought Spent. But Pester made a final move. "You have trouble with reality, Spent," he said. "You have trouble with what we philosophers call 'facta.'"

Spent took the comment as concession of defeat. He pushed his face into Pester's. "Forget your fucking facta, Anselm, and get out of my door. I have some drinking to do."

A classic barnyard riposte, it left Pester speechless. He twisted the key viciously. The door opened. Spent went in as Pester retreated down the hall.

Spent found himself sitting at his desk playing back the game. It called for a toast. He took his bottle of Wild Turkey out of the file cabinet, took a reassuring nip, then began reading test papers. They were preliterate scrawlings, as usual. Despair suddenly overwhelmed him. He scratched in his journal:

> The day drags like a mephitic slug across a sticky plank.... What a droll contrivance, the day. There is no need for days to be so long. All it would have taken is a measure of mercy, a trifle more spin on the planet at the birth of the world...

Unable to withstand any more of the papers, Spent went to the cafeteria for iced tea and a sweet roll. The tea was bitter and the bowl of communal sugar—sugar packets had priced themselves out of the market—was fouled with coffee stains. Most fitting, he thought, to this chicken yard of learned gentlemen. He thought of the elegance of the Quad Club out at the University of Chicago, of his days on the Chicago campus as a graduate student.

But he did not luxuriate long in those memories. Jenny Perch, supple, steaming, a divorcee in her early thirties, now Puffit's head secretary, came in and sat with him as she sipped a Coke.

"Hi. Am I bushed," she said.

"Hot as hell," said Spent.

"Oh, I'll be all right, but without air conditioning it's a problem. Those architects that put all those windows in that don't open should be hung. Architects are nuts, you know that? Crazy. But some men can't do anything right. All thumbs. I married a guy like that once. Five thumbs on each hand. That's ten thumbs in all. Like making love on cobblestones."

Spent had never noticed before just how beautiful Perch was. Her face was plain, her nose too broad and her jaw weak. But as she sat there, her bosom swelling like some great oceanic force, Spent knew she would never seem ordinary again.

She slumped in her chair. "God, I'm tired," she said as she slowly spread her legs until her skirt was taut. It was enough to derange Buddha in a trance.

Spent commented on the weather again. "The sweet rolls sure get sticky on a day like this."

Perch coiled an ankle round the leg of her chair as she teased the collar of her blouse with her fingers, long, scarlet-tipped, sensitive-looking. "You got something there, Cass," she said.

Spent repeated the comment, laughing slightly to let her know he was not above small talk.

She stared at him as if he had grown another nose. He was out on a limb. She casually sawed it off. "Nice talkin', professor," she said as she got up. "Don't go limp in the heat."

Spent stared at the soot-stained ceiling of the cafeteria. The noisy philosophizing of a cluster of FSU graduate degree candidates echoed from nearby tables. "The fuck you say, man!" Then, "No crap? No shit? Really, man?" Then, "She's some kind of snatch. She'll dive on it, man. A *real* coed!" Then, "No shit? Really?" It was the untrammeled pursuit of truth.

But as Spent sat there and the thought that he would be gone in the fall crept over him, the ugly, stumpy-looking creatures swirling about in filthy jeans seemed less revolting. And for an instant they became almost handsome, even beautiful, amendments to poor dead Darwin's vision of the brutish ape.

Spent's eyes drifted out onto the Plaza of Inspirations, where clusters of shirtless students lounged about sunning themselves. Most of them were playing cards. One small band had gathered about a pair of young men locked in a kicking, gouging, shive-flashing fight. Cheers erupted as one tried to mortally wound the other. Other students, mostly couples, seemed to be having sex, or encounters as yet unnamed by psychiatry, amongst the great mounds of waste that had accumulated around the bases of the concrete high-rises. Candy wrappers, crushed beer cans, plastic cups, snags of glistening plastic—evidently used condoms, from what Spent could tell—and discarded notebooks piled up, layer upon trampled layer.

The mounds of litter appeared three years ago when the groundskeeping staff was threatened by a student mob that had been enlisted to join a recycling drive. The drive ended abruptly when the president of the faculty senate, a perfumed sociologist who swept about the campus in flared French blue slacks—the blue intended to celebrate his lifelong devotion to Emile Durkheim's critique of religion—addressed a crowd of students on the steps of FSU's administration building. He denounced the recycling effort. He said it was a blatant effort by FSU's president "to reimpose the anal-retentive values of the Protestant ethic on the student body." He urged the students to take direct action. Most were too anesthetized from drugs. Only a small band of them rioted, lethargically. They managed to corner and severely beat but one official of the university, the Vice-President for Remaining Affairs. They let him loose, bloodied but smiling gratefully, when he informed the leader of the mob that he was part of America's rich new ethnic tapestry, that he was, in point of fact, Chuchi-Siberian.

But for all of the uplift and excitement of the display on the Plaza of Inspirations, Spent could not keep his mind off Jenny Perch, those thighs, velvety, opulent, bursting from under that tiny skirt, that tiny veil, so tentative, so provisional. He found himself shackled by his speculations, like a convict chained in solitary, like Saint Genet, poor wretch, squatting without hope in the corner of his shadowy prison cell, scalded with desire, one great, swollen, envious gland. And Spent began to tremble at the thought of what he might do to Perch to prove he was not just anybody. But in that desperate moment he bowed his neck to the iron law of futility. He did what any man of learning would do. He poured the remainder of his iced tea into the ashtray and watched the dirty little butts revolve as he stirred them with a straw. Why is the truth intrinsically sad, he asked himself, quoting hapless Renan. He could find no answer.

His eyes drifted out toward the concrete high-rises once again. When they were built he learned later, they had been the recipient of the Postmodern Architectural Metaphor of the Year award from the PMAIA, an eastern organization that had splintered off from the American Institute of Architects in 1987. The award had read:

> The buildings at Freedom State University are consciously down to earth, unapologetically mean and drab. They are the physical embodiment of the spirit of a great urban university. They capture the significant metaphor of our time. Their architects have succeeded masterfully. There is nothing to compare with it outside East Berlin.

Back in his office, how Spent was tested. How he was stretched, pulled, drawn, tugged and hauled through the enfeebling day by the impenitent hour hand of the clock.

His migraine struck again. It laid open his brain like a meat cleaver driven all the way down to the limbic stem. He took a drink of Wild Turkey, then tried to burrow beneath the stump of what was left of his cognition. He began to see double, then a haze hung over everything.

"Merde," he said decisively, and headed for a bar called The Heist. Immediately the hurricane in his head began to quiet. "Decisiveness," he thought. "The world needs decisiveness."

The Heist was a dark, quiet, inviting place where the air conditioner still hummed. The bar's owner had slipped the police a payoff.

The Heist celebrated Chicago at its cultural zenith. The walls were hung with pictures of famous gangsters and the old cars they used in gang wars. The waitresses were usually dressed as gun molls, in skirts and berets. The table lamps were converted sawed-off shotguns with lights protruding from the barrels. The place had elegance—oblique perhaps, but elegance nonetheless.

Violet Fromel worked in The Heist in the late afternoon and evening. She was a small, blonde woman, her hair piled high on her head, sprayed, neat and precise, in the fashion then favored in Cicero, where she grew up. Her nose was straight and refined, and her eyes were the color of amber. When Spent first saw her she reminded him of one of the small porcelain dolls his father had once given his mother in a vain effort to puncture the hatchet head's forbidding realism.

Fromel's English was not the best. Her "It don't make no difference" put Spent off a bit. But her makeup was as impressive as her hairdo. And when she was near the fluorescent lights glowing from under the bar, she took on an iridescent look, bringing to mind a kabuki dancer. It was something new in makeup, Spent realized. But he told himself there was more to life than questions of chemicals in a lady's makeup. Besides, he told himself, in the low light there were no blemishes, no moles, no pores, in fact—only soft, silken loveliness and the presence of her splendid perfume. It was evidence to Spent that progress might just still be possible.

Spent knew that Violet was in love with him. He had confirmed the fact by painstaking analysis and one small, brief concession to technology. He used a stopwatch to measure the time she spent at his table between service to other customers. On a typical data run he had five or six drinks, the stopwatch in his lap beneath the table. And when he finally tallied the data, they left his heart pounding. She did hang about more than she would have had to. She did care. She loved him!

My first marriage might still be alive and well if Delores had cared as much, Spent thought to himself as he had another Chivas to celebrate his flush of triumph. But Delores never gave a damn. Got out on a limb with stars in my eyes, made a move. She sawed it off, with a single calculated insult. *You fully Spent tonight, Casper, or only almost Spent?* Such women were born with a saw in one hand. And sitting there in front of the TV eating Twinkies and Ho-Ho's by the hour... arms shaped like dachshunds. She stepped out of one of Botero's paintings directly into my life, at eighteen.

The marriage foundered in a kettle of Crisco and recrimination.

On the way home that night, Spent thought how fortunate a man would be with a wife like Violet. She was simple, uncomplicated, unspoiled by thinking. There were practical considerations, too. With Vi at his side he might go into the tavern business. He could work the bar, and she the tables. He would have plenty of time for writing in the morning, after the kegs were tapped and the first steady customers came in at eighty-thirty for their pick-me-ups.

Violet and he would have a place rather like Kunst's, but instead of the huge mural of the Indians canoeing up the side of the wall, he would have a waterfront alehouse, something from out of the old classics, with brick walls, heavy tables and chairs, and an oak door three inches thick, a place where shifty-eyed adventurers would meet to study maps of lost treasure ships. Such men don't drink and run. They buy round after free-hearted round in heavy stoneware mugs. And even as they weave homeward they sing with Tom Paine, "The grateful pride of truth knows no extremes, and preserves in every latitude of life the right-angled character of man."

Spent drew out his journal and made a sketch again. Some day he would give it to Violet Fromel and she would understand the kind of man that went by the name of Casper Martin Spent.

And when the train passed beyond Gary and plunged into the wooded coves and swampy backlands of the dunes, through the hidden meadows aglow with lupine, Spent's spirits rose. Those were the secret places where he walked so often on Sunday afternoons to chew a sprig of sassafras and remember the homemade root beer he'd had as a child.

Last Sunday, when he was walking there, he saw a deer move quietly along the rise of a field swaying with milk-weed pods that had just begun to fill out. And he saw an indigo bunting, brilliant as a blue star, shining among the great green leaves of a basswood. He had thought all the indigo buntings were dead. He looked up and spoke to it. "You, sir," he said, "are a wonderful, redeeming apparition."

The bunting cocked its head and said to Spent, "How kind of you, dear friend. But I am real. I am the last of my kind." Then it broke for the higher limbs. As it did so it emitted a single long cry of anguish, touched with a note of thanks to Spent.

CHAPTER 6

By the end of February Spent was desperate. He prepared another memorandum for Puffit. This too, he vowed, would be crisp and unambiguous. It was initialed and signed with the unicorn, as usual.

February 27, 1997

To: Thomas Alvin Puffit
Dean, School of Education

From: Casper Martin Spent
Assistant Professor

Re: Reconsideration

Sir, consider what great men have done in the name of reconsideration. Consider the question of size. This universe, this earth, this flint and acid pit that God spit out after he masticated an eternity will forever remain mysterious. Think of the impious astrophysicist alone in his observatory late at night, doing calculations. He hunches like Faust, coveting omniscience with his Papermate pen. He moves red light one notch to the right on his spectograph. Lo! The spirit

> of old Chris Doppler materializes at his elbow. He stampedes the universe. Berenice whirls among the silver galaxies. Saturn pirouettes like sweet Pavlova in the purple night. His smugness is arrested with handcuffs of wonder.
>
> Sir, never let this be lost from mind. Reconsideration is a form of assertion. It is not weakness. It is born, like other deeds of valor, in lightning-torn clouds of fear and doubt. It tumbles as blue salvation from the hills of generosity. It makes the brown, sere world of distrust bloom beneath an ardent sun of friendship and inspiration. It turns our spirit green. It makes us quake in anticipation, like the gentle aspen. It restores our love of men. It wets our spirit's whistle. It retreats to its divine home only when life has been set on its course again, throbbing with resolution. Then it withdraws quietly, like a doting mother leaving the bedroom of her tiny, sleeping, thumb-sucking son.

Confident that his memo would slam into Puffit like a *J'accuse* thunderbolt from Zola, Spent headed for The Heist.

It was three o'clock in the afternoon. The temperature was up again, hovering in the nineties. Along Michigan Avenue paperboys hawked a special edition of the *Tribune*. Many wore white surgical masks like those popularized in Peking in the eighties. The masks helped filter the stench coming up from the sewers. The headlines read SNOWS SEEN IN KATMANDU. The story announced another presidential reassurance. Citizens were told that the nation's leading scientists were looking into this "present and, we believe, transient matter of the atmosphere."

Spent pushed aside the paperboy and ducked into The Heist. He moved past the bar, took a chair near a side table and ostentatiously opened his briefcase. He took out his journal and began making notes.

"My, you're a busy bee, today," said Violet as she came

up to him, whirling her small service tray balanced on the tips of her fingers. She was dressed in a small, fluffy white blouse and a pair of white short-shorts with cuffs. Spent caught his breath. He had always been attracted to women dressed in white—nurses, waitresses, beauticians, even lab technicians. They looked clean and fresh, but very tangible, as if they were gift-wrapped by a minimalist, and eager to be unwrapped. He never found glamor and sophistication appealing. In fact, it put him off. Too much attention to the outside could only mean chill and self-denial on the inside. And then too there was always that mysterious prepossessing quality of the color white. Within it the rainbow lay hidden.

"Get ya a drink?" she asked.

Spent ordered a double Chivas and returned to his notes, letting the girl's curiosity get the best of her.

"Don'tcha know you shouldn't take the office home with you? Ain't good for your health. 'Specially in this weather."

Spent put his journal aside with mock impatience. "If you insist."

"I got a riddle for you. I know ya like riddles. You told me when ya had a load, last week."

"All of life is a riddle."

"What's a sad case?"

Spent was baffled. He shrugged. "I give up. I surrender. I'm yours."

"A dozen empties," she giggled. "Gotcha good, didn't I?"

"You sure did. Got me good." He erupted in a loud, superfluous laugh that startled Violet.

"It ain't *that* funny," she said. "But I gotta lot of 'em. They're off our new bar napkins. You ain't seen 'em yet. Ted didn't put 'em out. Wants to surprise customers later today when there's more of 'em in here."

"Just what the world needs," said Spent. "More bar napkin jokes."

"Some is really cute. Like, 'What are smelling salts?'" She waited. "Well?"

"Stumped again. What?"

"Sailors that need showers."

Spent laughed too hard again.

"Boy, you sure go for riddles," she said. Then, eyeing his empty glass, "Need to freshen your drink?"

"Sure. Another double. Then I got to go."

"I can tell you like to toss a few off. Whenever I hear a guy say he's got to go, I know he's gonna have at least two more."

Spent could feel himself flush. His father had always ordered his next round with a "Then I got to go."

The waitress said, "Oh, just kiddin', for Pete's sake. I enjoy a few drinks too, y'know."

Spent said, "It'll have to be a quickie."

"Wish I could have a quickie," she said giggling, her hands fluttering over her hairdo. "I mean a drink, not the other kind of quickie. But them's good too." She pretended to cover a blush. "Hungry as a wolf, though."

Spent made his move. "Well, I have no excuse for that. I had a splendid lunch. One might even say the quintessential lunch."

"*What* kind of lunch? One of them new things, some kind of supersub sandwich?"

"No, just a fine lunch at Renoir's. He let the name slide off easily, as if Chicago's finest was a mere hamburger stand.

Her response was right on the money. "It's kinda expensive, ain't it?"

He shrugged.

"Go there often?"

Spent knew he had his foot planted squarely on the

bottom rung. "Well, yes and no. When my appointment calendar requires a quiet place with a distinguished menu. I go there when business makes it necessary, whether I'm out of town or not."

The pressure was showing. The out-of-town line almost ended it. But she blamed the Chivas. "Well, you can't eat at Renoir's when you're out of town, can you?"

He regrouped. "You certainly have a mind like a steel trap, Miss Violet." A little humor and the realization that he had traveled in the south could not hurt.

She found the "Miss Violet" very funny, and she laughed her small tinkling laugh with its odd little wheeze at the end. But she suspected Spent was putting her on. She turned as if to walk away, then shot a glance at him. "What d'ya do for a livin'?"

"Oh, I'm just a professor. A professor of philosophy," he said.

"Wow," she said. "You must know a lot."

"That's a philosopher's business, to know a lot, and sometimes to try to forget a lot. And, of course, to use what we remember wisely."

"University of Chicago is a wonderful school, ain't it? Even if a lot of creeps hang around out there on the Midway, twinkle-toe types. I see them over the wall. I ride the I.C. You must be in their downtown center, over on Lake. I seen you walking there the other day. My brother goes to FSU, across the bridge, on Wabash."

"I know about FSU," said Spent.

Violet rattled on. "It's a pretty shitty place. But he wanted to study cookin'. He tried to get cookin' at Chicago. They told him they didn't offer it, except out at the Argonne National Laboratory. The guy said they cook up a lot out there. But he didn't make much sense to my brother. Least my brother is gettin' an education at FSU finally. He went to school, sorta, out at Joliet Penitentiary for a while, but it was the wrong kind, if ya know what I mean." She giggled again. "I never went to no school after high school. I guess that means no school at all. Right? So here I am."

"Well, we're all someplace, Miss Violet," Spent said. "But Chicago is a fine school."

"Must be if they got to put a wall around it to keep the animals out. Wish I could walk around there some time and see it all. They put up some new buildings even with this depression goin' on."

"A great university."

"Oh there's got to be some smart profs out there. Gotta be. Like that economist guy. Swedes gave him a medal for being noble. He's on TV a lot. Little round face. Smiles when he's mad. He says Hong Kong is where it's happening. They built a new kind of harbor there he says, from the old cathouses, after the water came up. Course, I never been to Hong Kong."

"A world city."

"Always thought it a seedy dump, judgin' from what the papers say. People drinkin' sewer water and things. Or paddlin' them junks around the harbor between the lumps of shit." She caught herself. "I mean, lumps of stuff. *You* know. Toilet stuff."

"I've heard the word," Spent grinned.

"I know, but philosophers don't use words like that... but if that economist is a famous man, and if he says drinkin' sewer water ain't all that bad... I just don't know."

"Economics is often called the dismal science."

"Well, if economists tell us turds in our drinkin' water is okay they can't be all that dismal." She caught herself again. "I shouldn't use them kinda words."

"You mean *economist?*"

"No, silly. I mean *turds*. She held a hand over her mouth. "There, I said it again." She laughed her tiny, enchanting laugh.

Violet was called back to the bar. She and the bartender, Ted Stoutbottom, were suddenly caught up in an intense, apparently heated exchange. Spent watched them for a few minutes, then, as the waitress turned her back on the bartender in a kind of sulk, he finished his drink and signaled for another. She brought it to him quickly, smiled and returned to the bar, frowning.

It was obvious to Spent that a fit of jealousy had all but overwhelmed the bartender. Stoutbottom glanced over toward Spent once or twice, then went back to work. He was an enormous man with a large massive head, balding down the middle, with a wide, heavy-lipped mouth. He balanced a huge paunch, upholstered in a brocade vest, as his small, fat hands fluttered among the glasses he was washing. His ponderous bulk moved with a kind of natural grace. That day he became "the Toad" in Spent's journal.

Violet Fromel was standing at Spent's table again. She could see his thoughts had strayed. "Hey!" she said, "the scotch puttin' ya to sleep?"

"No," he said, and ordered another.

"Never liked scotch myself," she said. "Tastes like smelly socks. Be right back, Cass."

"How did you know my name?" he asked when she returned with the drink.

"Oh I'm quite a detective."

"Oh?"

"Sure. You cashed a check here last month. 'Member? For twenty dollars. You were pretty high. Said I had a beautiful nose. I said you weren't exactly standing behind the door when the Lord handed yours out either. But I like big noses on men, big feet, too." She laughed. "That ape behind the bar didn't want to take the check. I told him you had a nice face. Maybe you could use a little more hair up on the dome, but you got a nice face. And 'Cass' is short for Casper, ain't it?"

It was then that Spent asked Violet Fromel to lunch with him at Boucher's, the restaurant at the art gallery. "Why, Cass, I'd love to," she squealed, "I'd just love to." She added, still squealing, but more quietly, "Course, some of them paintings leave me cold. We can skip that, can't we?" And he had told her of course, that paintings were more or less irrelevant to the whole idea of a postmodern gallery. It was good company and whispered witticisms that counted.

The dull ride home that evening scarcely seemed to matter to Spent.

When Spent got home, Dorothy and Swag were drinking beer and carrying on about the wonders of the future that lay just around the corner for them as soon as Swag got enough money to buy a truck and go into business for himself. Swag was saying, "I'm gonna get me one of them big babies with hydraulic lifts so's I can tailgate gravel. Lotsa people around here need their drives graveled. I'd say most of 'em do. Life can be hell if your drive ain't graveled."

And Dorothy was saying, "And you know what I'm gettin' outta this deal? A new flower garden, just like in *House and Garden* magazine. Tiger lilies, dahlias, gladiolas. All shimmering in God's lovely sunshine—and unafraid to accept His love."

Swag was sitting in his undershirt, cross-legged on the floor, his shoes off, his five o'clock shadow giving his handsome face the swarthy look of a Bolivian bandit. He was fixing the vacuum cleaner. The boys had used it outside in the grass, trying to find the cotter pin from the axle of their wagon. Dorothy was sitting on the sofa, brushing her hair, as she did whenever she sat on the sofa. She was in her housecoat, despite the heat.

"Have a beer, Cass," Swag boomed when his brother-in-law pushed through the front door.

"Need a shower," said Spent wearily.

"The kids are in there now, brother. Timmy and Kenny is havin' a ball. Hear 'em? Little beggars are sure happy today. They been in there for an hour."

Spent retreated to his room. He undressed and sat in his reading chair as he waited.

His room was swarming with houseflies. He watched them for a few minutes, his bile rising. They whizzed about him like dashing aeronauts, some, it seemed to Spent, in white silk scarves and goggles, doing loops and strafing runs as they worked him over.

He had complained often to Swag about the rusted-out screen on his window. But it was hopeless. Now, without winter, the damn flies never let up. Only a cold, subzero blast could bring them down a peg or two. Spent got up, swatted at the flies futilely with his undershirt. He finished off what was left of the bottle of Canadian Club he kept under a pile of socks he had tried, for over a year, to get his sister to darn. Then he trapped one of the flies in the empty bottle. "Inhale it, you little shit!" he said. "Get a good whiff. We'll see how good those high-tech compound eyes are." He loosed the fly a foot from the wall. The insect came out roaring, engine at full throttle, all courage and no foresight, in an elegant slow turn. He hit the wall and Spent executed it without trial, on the floor, with a single swat of his shoe.

Forty minutes later, Spent got into the shower. He emerged refreshed, intent on telling Dorothy and Swag about Violet Fromel's love for him.

Dinner, as usual, was constant chatter from the kids and another guessing game. This time Swag insisted that Spent try to guess why the kids were so keyed up.

Finally it came out. Swag had traded several wrenches and a power drill that needed a new chuck for a pair of rabbits. He had been at Werner Kunst's tavern most of the day. When he threw in the wrenches, the deal was closed. He spent the rest of the afternoon building a hutch for the rabbits, out behind the garage. The boys were beside themselves with joy and insisted that Uncle Cass bolt his German potatoes and franks so he could go out to see their pets.

There they were, behind the screen, nibbling primly at the grass the boys had stuffed into the cage. Timmy demanded that his uncle join in pulling up grass and clover.

"One's a buck, the other's a girl!" said Swag. "Cute little varmints, ain't they? Cute enough to eat," he teased. "Maybe we could have 'em for dinner tomorrow night?" Timmy punched his dad playfully in the stomach.

But the jest was not lost on Spent. A flash of inventiveness struck him. He had an inspiration. And this time it was not an ordinary inspiration. It was the kind of thing the unicorn would understand. He drew Swag aside and told him he wanted to confer immediately, without the kids around, and with Dorothy, on the porch, over a beer, while the kids stayed with their rabbits.

Dorothy caught his sense of urgency. She told the boys to stay and search for a four-leaf clover. She said rabbits grew fat and fluffy as teddy bears if they were fed four-leaf clovers. Then she hurried off for the beer.

Swag, Spent and Dorothy made themselves comfortable on the porch. They sat in the old white plastic lawn chairs; he sat on the steps.

"Swag," Spent began. "You know anything about hasenpfeffer?"

"'Course I know about hasenpfeffer," Swag said impatiently. "You're lookin' at a man called Swagmacher, for Christ's sake."

"Well, it's a delicacy, you know that. Your mother's recipe for it would make Hermann Goering do a barrel roll in his grave."

"Now, wait a minute, Cass," Swag said. "The kids love them rabbits. We ain't about to kill those fuzzy little fellas to make no damn delicacy."

"Now just hold yourself in check a moment," Spent reassured his brother-in-law. "I do not propose killing those two rabbits. I propose breeding them systematically. Do you realize what we have here, Swag?" He waited for an answer. Swag shook his head. "We have seed stock."

"Seed stock? What in hell is seed stock?"

Spent explained what seed stock meant in the animal breeding business. Then he went further, backing his case with scientific data. He got out the *World Book,* volume eight in the used edition Swag had bought the boys, and noted that the domestic hare, *Oryctolagus cuniculus,* has no fixed period in its breeding cycle. Gestation lasts a month, and six to eight young are born to each litter. Then the female resolutely becomes pregnant again.

To clinch his case, Spent got pencil and paper and made a few quick calculations. He showed that in ten generations, a single pair of rabbits could produce precisely 120,936,352 rabbits, plus or minus a few dozen because of problems of sterility or heat stroke. "And now that we have no seasons, Swag," Spent added as the clincher, "We can double that number, roughly, plus or minus..."

Both Dorothy and Swag were stunned. They had not been exposed to the principle of an exploding universe before. "Holy balls," said Swag reverently.

"Now no need to be vulgar, honey," Dorothy said.

And Swag, staring into the distance, said, "I don't mean it that way, Dorth. I just mean that's one hell of a lot of rabbits."

Spent rode the tide. "Swag, do you realize what this means because of the trouble in the beef business? With T-bones going at thirty-four dollars a pound? It means if you have quality rabbits, you have quality hasenpfeffer. If you have quality hasenpfeffer, you have money in the bank. And we retire those two pets out there without ever having to skin the little critters. The kids keep their pets. Everybody's happy!"

"Cass," said Swag, "you're usually full of crap. But on this one you may be right—if your figures are right."

Spent went through the mathematical exercise again, demonstrating the hard, immutable laws of deductive reasoning. "You see, Swag," he went on, leading his brother-in-law gently into the facts of life about the business world, "you have got to learn to reason simply and directly, without frills, straight from one thing to another. Rabbits, hasenpfeffer, money. Most people have difficulty seeing things that clearly. But the key to success in the business world is, stay simple! And when the right moment comes, make your move—one, two, three. It's all a matter of timing."

"Yeah," said Swag. "I heard lots of people talkin' about the importance of timing in things like this. I guess you got to make your move at just the right time. You gotta let the soft underbelly of the thing crystallize, then move!" He pounded his fist into his palm.

Spent went on. "My boy, we have our toe in the door of the rabbit ranching business. If there's one thing a rabbit likes more than cabbage, it's another rabbit."

Dorothy giggled. "There's no doubt about it, Cass. It's a fine opportunity. It could help a lot. You know we need the extra money."

Her brother cautioned, "Prudence, of course, will need to be exercised. We will have to begin by buying land for more hutches. And, of course, the hutches themselves will be expensive. And it will take a lot of work."

"Work?" Swag asked. "Work? Who in hell's afraid of a little work? I'm not. Dorth's not. You're not. So we made a smart move, that's all."

Spent said, "We'll need a loan... from the bank."

Swag's jaw sagged. "How in hell would we keep up if we don't? In no time this whole place will be swarming with rabbits. Just the cost of wood and screen could run into a pretty penny. Them hutches will cover acres. Getting that kind of money ain't easy." He paused, scratched his head and said, "It's hard to get to see the top guy in them banks. They know a good thing when they see it, but you got to get past that secretary. You gotta get into the inner sanction."

Spent told Swag he would photograph the rabbits as soon as the first litters were born. He said the pictures would be solid evidence of the vitality of their breeding stock, the kind of thing a hardheaded banker would demand.

Dorothy leaned back in her chair. "I knew it. I just knew it. Swag, honey, you and Cass are two fine men... and full of imagination, and full of what this country represents. You're fine Americans, both of you."

Dorothy's tender comments sent Spent's mind spinning back toward Violet Fromel. She, too, would be impressed, especially with her brother studying cooking at FSU. Even Puffit might take notice. Finally the wood duck would get the break it deserved. Off and flying, fast, like a shot, the way a wood duck always does, cutting a fine, low trajectory through forests of irresolution and imbecility.

The sun was going down and the air had cooled. The boys were still playing with the rabbits. Spent could hear them laughing out near the hutch.

Swag was caught up in the beauty of the moment. He dashed into the house and came out with the transistor radio. "Now how about a little music on the subject?" He fiddled with the radio. A news bulletin was being pumped out of Washington. "... this news special. President Kempt announced today that he will be traveling to Chile next month to confer with President Horta y Gassett. The summit will concern a bilateral agreement permitting the United States to put in place a high-technology system for ventilating the earth's heat through the polar hole in the Van Allen radiation belt. New mass-driver laser pulse systems are to be used. The president was quoted as saying..."

Swag switched to another station. "More of that same politics bull," he said. "Kempt don't know his ass from a goal line." A puke rock hit came blaring in from KTTT in Hammond.

Dorothy covered her ears. "Not that music, dear, pleeeease," she pleaded. "Find some of the old stuff, from Lombardo."

Swag looked puzzled.

"You know, honey," said Dorothy, "the guy that played the sax. They built that big memorial for him up in Canada, at the resort on Baffin Island. The resort our government helped get built next to them factories that make oil from sandy tar."

"Guy Lombardo!" said Swag, bursting into a grin. "Hell, yes. Your favorite, right, honey?"

"That's him, dear. His music is so wonderful, so unafraid. I love it, just lu-u-ve it. But they hardly ever broadcast him anymore."

Dorothy's admiration for things unafraid was evidence of her growing anxiety about what the change in the weather might mean for the future of her kids. She had grown anxious deep inside herself, where her most elemental maternal instincts lay, where her most ancient primate intuitions operated. They told her that something in the world was seriously wrong. Her response was to steady herself by reaching for some favorite memory, some bit of nostalgia, anything that would stand still in a world turned upside down. For Dorothy, Lombardo had joined the immortals. He had gone beyond uncertainty.

Swag sensed the depth of Dorothy's worries. "I know you love old Guy's music, honey. You just love it for all it's worth. We all need something, besides each other and the kids and old Cass here." He got up from his chair, walked down off the porch and turned around slowly, staring at the sky. "This hasenpfeffer thing is a big idea, Cass," he said. "Bigger than even you or I realize. Hell, we ain't even scratched the horizon of the possibilities," he said dreamily.

Dorothy took the radio in her lap and twisted the dial back and forth. Static hissed and popped across the dial. "Must be one of them satellites busted again," she said. "Every time one of those new ones go on the fritz it spoils everything."

Then the static cleared. Puke rock blared from one end of the dial to the other, except for the small evangelist station broadcasting out of the Michigan City State Prison. "Oh lamb of God, please come... please come," it blared into the twilight.

Chapter 7

It was just after twelve noon when Violet Fromel and Casper Spent met at Boucher's patio restaurant at the art gallery. Spent's eyes widened when he saw his date. It was the first time he had seen her in daylight. Her makeup was especially striking. Her eyes were deeply shadowed with chic ocher tones and her lips were layered with a wet, glistening, gunmetal gray lipstick. She wore a small red frock that fell just off the shoulders, and on her feet she wore fashionable ankle-high boots soled with heavy pieces of auto tire, disdainfully referred to by the traditionalist fashion editors as "Third World pumps."

Spent himself cut a distinctive figure. He wore a three-piece polyester suit known, though somewhat derogatorily, as "Sears Revival." It was cut along lines made popular in the seventies by the golf star Johnny Miller. Spent set it off with a dusty blue shirt and a club tie with small red helicopters against a navy blue field.

The *fête galante* atmosphere of the vestibule to the restaurant impressed Violet. In fact, it all but bowled her over. Against the heavy velour wallpaper hung two large copies of paintings on view in the upstairs galleries. Both were in postmodern allegorical style. One showed Jupiter salivating over Antiope. She lay in a sleepy, unapologetic sprawl, exposing herself with the gynecological candor of a 1980s' *Playboy* centerfold. The other was Leda and the Swan. A creamy Leda lay on a mossy forest floor. The swan, full of priapic pride but vexed by the uncertainties of anatomical compatibility, loomed above her.

Violet loved the paintings. "Boy, Cass," she said in an excited whisper, "those broads look experienced. And that swan's been around, that's for damn sure. Look at its eyes! What do those funny lookin' little TV screens reflecting in 'em mean?"

Spent gave her a playful squeeze. "It's in the manner of Boucher," he said. "His colors remind people of rosc petals floating in milk."

They alerted the maître d' to their presence and took seats on two of the heavily upholstered, cabriole-legged chairs set along the wall near the entrance to the patio. Violet's eyes swept the room excitedly. Next to her a flowering crab clung precariously to life in a small pot enameled in the T'ien style. And beside it stood a small bronze statue of a nude boy sexually molesting a goat.

A gentleman who seemed particularly proud of his nostrils showed them to their table.

The garden restaurant sparkled with life. The chattering patrons were clustered in twos and threes and fours at the tables under large yellow parasols. Heavy black wrought-iron table legs shone with stubborn elegance from beneath white plastic tablecloths. The sky was brilliant blue, almost cloudless. The bronze dolphins in the reflecting pool stood proudly on their tails, spraying jets of water from their mouths. It fell shimmering into the pool, turning the sky's reflection into a giant patch of splintered blue crystal.

The patio's sculpture was boldly eclectic, though two monumental pieces from the seventies dominated everything about them. One was by an artist from Waco, much admired during his career for his sense of space. It consisted of a giant pile of empty oil drums, an unflinching if somewhat poignant statement.

"Glad we ain't sittin' near that thing," said Violet, pointing a thumb over her shoulder toward the oil barrels. "That damn pile ever lets go, it'll iron a couple of these people into the floor like they were in a Saturday morning cartoon."

Spent assured her that it was held together by nuts and bolts they couldn't see. There was no way, he said, that a curious hand or tipsy foot could send the barrels rampaging through the happy colony of lunching art lovers.

Violet was relieved. "But that one over there don't look much safer," she said, pointing to a thirty-foot-long concrete sewer pipe, artfully shattered at its upper end and sunk at a frightening angle into a giant plinth of raw concrete.

"Pieces of that period emphasized the play of kinetic forces," said Spent, "hence your unsettled feeling."

"Suppose so," said Violet. She laughed. "Bet I can guess its name. *Sewer Pipe?*"

"No," said Spent leaning back in his chair, almost pompously. "It's entitled *Ode to Mr. Daley and the Building Trades.* It's famous now, all over the country. When they were installing it, the artist made a mistake and it tipped over and killed him."

"Misjudged the kinetic forces, Cass?" Violet asked innocently.

"As a matter of fact, he did," said Spent expansively. "Fact is, they never found part of one of his feet after the accident. It's in there in the cement base, somewhere near the bottom. The concrete set while they were hauling him to the hospital. That's why the work has such a bittersweet title."

Spent was pontificating and enjoying it. He enjoyed letting Violet know that he knew something about the arts, even though contemporary art put him off. He considered it proof of the collapse of good sense as well as sensibility, evidence, in fact, of the corrupt spirit of his times. But being with Violet made it all seem more meaningful, even necessary.

Their eyes met and for a moment did not move. They smiled. Spent ordered double daiquiris.

When the drinks arrived they each took a heavy first sip as their eyes locked once again.

Violet's eyes drifted toward the pool. "Just love daqs," she said.

"Mmmmmmmm," said Spent, lengthening his second sip.

"And I just love this place," she said. "I just love learning about art. I'd never know what to name that sewer pipe. I really wouldn't."

She studied the two large plates set before them, then gasped, "And just *look* at these plates, Cass! This is somethin'."

The rims of the plates were decorated with elements taken from Judy Chicago's famed *Dinner Party,* mostly small, pink abstractions of female reproductive parts, mounds, folds and intriguing crevices.

"They're from a tour de force of the seventies," said Spent. "Judy Chicago's *Dinner Party.* Meant to raise public consciousness... about the true meaning of being a woman."

"Wanted people to know we're more than just moving parts, right Cass?" asked Violet. Then she frowned. "I ain't so sure though, Cass. Look at this one here. See? Looks like the panic button to me. That thing don't raise consciousness, not really." She caught herself. "Oh, my God," she said. "There I go again. Got to learn to keep my big mouth shut."

Spent chuckled. "Raising consciousness can be a touchy matter," he said.

His date, stifling her laugh, doubled up and almost fell from her chair. "My God, Cass," she wheezed, "now *you're* doin' it."

Then she became serious as her gaze fell on the reflecting pool. "When I was a kid, we used to sneak into the parks and swim in them fountains. The cops was always after me. We had fish spittin' water like that, too. But now the city's shut them all down. Stunk too much. Somethin' in the pipes I guess—rats or somethin'. They shut Buckingham down because of rats, that big beautiful fountain right out there in Grant Park behind us. Wonder why this one's still goin'?"

Violet's question was not meant to be answered so Spent didn't.

They ordered sandwiches, BLTs. They were a treat for Violet. The price of bacon was as high as that of lobster, and the lobster was more-or-less extinct.

As they ate their sandwiches, Spent's eyes dwelt on Violet's shoulders, on her throat, then on her tiny earlobes. Her makeup didn't look as it had in The Heist. But it was still satiny and chatoyant despite her perspiration, still a marvel of postmodern chemistry. And beneath it he knew a woman existed, with a heart that throbbed and a pulse that beat. He could feel himself falling in love.

Violet wanted to know if Spent was married. He told her he had been but that the marriage fell apart because of his wife's narrow-minded attitude about their having to take long winter vacations with his mother so she could attend the snowmobile races in Hayward, Wisconsin. He seemed suddenly sad to Violet. "That was all back in the days when we had ice on the lakes at this time of year."

She grew serious, too. "I was married to a creep." Her shoulders shook with a mock shudder. "He was really something. Came from a little burg in Maine. We had to pray every time we did it. You imagine that? I had to teach the saphead everything. I mean *everything!*"

But with their second drinks, Violet began uncorking her napkin riddles. "What's a will, Cass? Give up?"

"Give up."

"A dead giveaway!" she said, doubling up with laughter.

Things were going so well that Spent told Violet that they should do it again some time.

"Do what?"

"Have lunch like this."

"At Renoir's, maybe? I'd love that, Cass. Just love it."

"They have wonderful food there," said Spent. "They specialize in Arctic dishes now, things that are big at the Yukon resorts, like crepes voyageur. It uses a pastry scented with the *merest* touch of rancid elk fat."

"Count me out on that one," said Violet.

"Well then, we can have their famous hasenpfeffer."

"What's that, for Pete's sake? And don't kid me."

Spent told Violet about hasenpfeffer and of Swag's mother's magnificent recipe for it. Then he told Violet about Swag and his rabbit-ranching business.

She was enthralled, her interest piqued. Gushing with excitement, she told Cass about her brother, Richie. "I got a brother that's studyin' cookin' at FSU. I think I told ya that. Well, he's flunkin' out. If he could come in with a good recipe, somethin' that would let his prof know how smart he is, it could save him." Her hand reached out to Spent's. "Oh, Cass, could I? Could I tell him? Could I give him your recipe? I know he could learn it. They got lots of tough things to learn at Freedom State."

Spent realized he had let the cat out of the bag. But it was not a cat, after all, upon which everything depended. It was a pair of rabbits, the private lives of *Oryctolagus cuniculus*. He said, "Of course you may, my dear." And he scribbled down the recipe he had committed to memory a week earlier.

Violet was ecstatic. "This'll save him, Cass. It really will. Rabbits are still pretty common. Like Ted Stoutbottom says, they ship them in from Australia now since their cattle ranches folded, like ours. Richie couldn't do anything with a beef recipe. Too expensive, but this rabbit thing . . . this hasen . . . pff . . ."

"Hasenpfeffer," said Spent.

"I'll call him from The Heist. Oh, Cass, I think you're the most wonderful, the kindest man."

Their eyes met again. "I'm beginning to feel you're not an ordinary anybody either, Miss Violet," said Spent. He called for the check and paid for lunch.

It was the unicorn that suggested to Spent that he not go right home when he reached Tremont later that day, so they walked to the lake. The sky was still cloudless. The sun hung low in the southwest. The air seemed to be flushed with blue-gold dust. Everything was still. The water was smooth, a frosted pane of blue-green glass. Spent and the unicorn walked up a high dune and sat, watching a solitary pair of kildeer wheeling in above the water and settling on the sand, then calling to one another as they took off to circle in the hush. There was an unseen bond between them, a silver thread of love.

Spent had not really been in love since he was fifteen. He had been infatuated—in love, after a fashion—with Deborah Fanview back in graduate school. But that was different. Fanview was a professor, which gave the whole thing a different twist. And she lifted weights, was a champion, in fact, in the clean and jerk, which for Spent seemed to complicate things.

Adeline was Spent's first real love. She was a Norwegian girl, living on her father's dairy farm ten miles from Spent's hometown. She was blonde, shy and beautiful. Whenever he saw her, usually when her parents came to town to shop, the memory of her would cling for days like a scented reverie. And once, one summer, when she was visiting a playmate in the village, he saw her at the swimming hole down by the dam. She was swimming by herself when he came upon her. She swam out to the diving platform and pulled herself up. She sat there for ten minutes, tanned, glistening in the sun. He knew she saw him standing on the bridge, but she pretended not to. Then she dived into the water and languidly sank to the bottom. She flexed her knees against the sand and catapulted up and out of the water, as strange and lovely as some mythic animal of the sea. He whispered "... animal of the sea. Wear pearls of sunlight in your hair as the gulls hover over you. You are Eve and I will always love you..."

And later that day, the boy climbed into a cottonwood and secretly carved her initials in the bark, high in the topmost boughs. Long after the cut healed he would climb the tree and let the scar cast its spell.

When winter came and ice skating began, two friends of Casper's, Jimmy and Roland, built their fire as usual on the old pine stump near the shore. The girls would show up to skate and he saw Adeline once again.

Jimmy and Roland never skated. They hung around the fire and teased the girls. But Spent and Adeline made a long trip up the lake behind the dam to a place where a narrow bridge kept patches of water open.

The ice in the narrows was always clear, and when they lay on it, with their coats over their heads, they could watch the sunlight playing on the bottom. The weeds were emerald green and moved slowly, blown by strange water winds. And then he and Adeline discovered a brilliant patch of speckled stone where perch hovered weightless in the eerie breeze. And near it they discovered a rotted hulk of a launch, faint traces of its white paint still visible on its heavy shiplap sides. They named it *Jenny*.

Spent made up a story about the launch. He said that in the old days, when the launch's great inboard engine roared and drove the boat across the lake to the elegant lawn parties of a rich man now dead, the brims of the huge hats of the lady passengers flapping in the wind, the launch sprang a leak. The wind rose suddenly and every life was threatened. It was only, he said, the bravery of the young skipper that saved the day. The skipper, Spent told Adeline, was his father.

Adeline and Casper agreed not to tell the others what they had found. And as they skated back to the fire, he held her hand. Long after the teasing stopped he could feel the warmth of her hand through his mitten.

In his bedroom late that night he stared out the dormer window. The Big Dipper hung inverted in the northern sky. It had become marvelously conspicuous to the boy.

The next day at school he studied the constellation in the big library dictionary, and at his desk he wrote sketches of several stories about what ancient mariners said when they first saw the Dipper turn upside down. Then he composed a poem to Adeline and mailed it to her unsigned.

I wear a vision on my brain
Her toes just touch a star
She dances sweetly in the night
And keeps my heart awake

Adeline's father, a big man who was drunk half the time and cursed Swedes and beat his cattle the rest of the time, intercepted the poem and forced his daughter to tell him everything Spent had said. Then he called Spent's mother. He threatened to "beat the tar out of that lying little whelp of yours if he ever goes near my girl again."

Spent's father understood. But the hatchet head did not. So Spent did the only thing left to him. He fell in love with a beautiful blonde girl living as a model in the undergarment section of the Montgomery Ward catalogue, on the same page as a small picture of a unicorn.

It was the unicorn's gentle nudge that reminded Spent that it was time to get home, to get on with his plans.

When Spent got home it was bedlam. Timmy and Kenny were bawling their eyes out. Dorothy was bedraggled with weeping, alternately consoling the boys and suppressing a shudder of tears.

At first Spent thought something had happened to Swag, but that was not it. The problem was more complicated. It was the rabbits, the ranching scheme. Kenny blubbered out the story.

The big lummox mongrel from the pony farm down the road had wandered over and proceeded to assault the seed stock. He knocked over the hutch, the roof came off, and when the rabbits bolted for freedom, he drove one under the porch of the house and killed the other, the male Toothy. When Timmy crawled under the porch to catch Fuzzy, she made a dash for the woods and disappeared into the underbrush. The boy's frantic effort to capture it merely drove it into deeper cover.

When Kenny finished the story and the final tear seemed shed, the boys begged for a funeral for Toothy. Spent was numb with shock, but went along. They found a Nabisco cracker box and laid Toothie out on a bed of crumpled toilet tissue. Spent dug the grave with one of Swag's shovels. Timmy found a brick to use as a headstone.

It was after dark by the time the burial service had begun. In the moonlight, Kenny knelt and began to pray. Dorothy, standing at the back door of the house, daubed her eyes, then hustled out to where Kenny was on his knees. "Honey," she said, pulling the boy to his feet, "You mustn't pray for animals. Only pagans pray for animals. We're not pagans. Ask Uncle Cass, dear. He's from the university. He knows about things like pagans. Besides, pagans are always so afraid."

Spent overruled his sister. "Dorothy, if we can eat the little devils, we can pray for them." He nodded to Kenny, and the pagan rite was completed.

Walking back to the house, Dorothy leaned on her brother's arm. "Oh, Cass," she said, her voice quivering on the verge of another sob, "the rabbits meant so much to all of us. They were the future, Cass, the future. All our hopes and plans gone, just gone. Everything was so wonderful. Now it's all gone. These are hard times, Cass, for everyone."

Swag arrived. When he heard what had happened, he immediately began laying plans to sue the dog's owner. The first thing, he said, was to go to Kunst's tavern. Werner Kunst would know how to go about it. But before they left they would make a final search for Fuzzy. "Line up in a row, ten feet apart. Cass and I on the ends with flashlights. We'll sweep the area. I seen police do it when they're lookin' for bodies."

They swept and swept for almost an hour. Fuzzy had disappeared for good.

When they returned to the house, Swag slumped onto the sofa. Timmy and Kenny, desolate, sat beside him. He reassured them, with a strong steady voice. "Look," he said, "I been all over this country. I seen it change. I seen it grow. I seen presidents come and go. We ain't goin' to let this thing get us down. We'll come up with something. You'll see. The future is always darkest before the dawn, like they say. I can tell you one thing. I'm an American through and through. And I got enough Kraut in me to make me tough. Despair ain't goin' to be no iron cross around my neck."

Spent went to his room, took off the shirt that was covered with burrs from the sweeping effort and put on a clean one. Then he took a long, attentive pull on his new bottle of Canadian Club. As the warmth of the amber fluid moved down his throat and settled in his stomach he studied the bottle's label with its crested seal and splendid phrasing of its distiller's license. "By Appointment to Her Majesty Queen Elizabeth II." He rejoined Swag and they drove in Spent's old Chevy, by royal appointment, as it were, slowly and very deliberately toward Kunst's tavern.

Swag was wound up and angry. The loss of the breeding stock had been a severe shock to him. He reminded Spent that the Swagmachers came from Prussia originally and that they were a family that cherished ancient values. "The German people ain't a very funny people, Cass," he said, "but they know how to get even. I ain't done yet, not by a damn site. I still got an ace up my hole, Cass."

Spent, now feeling the warmth of his royal appointment all the way down to his shoe soles, doubled up in laughter, drove off the road through a shallow ditch and came up against a burr oak. "*In* the hole," he wheezed. "*In* the hole."

Swag got out of the car, walked around to the driver's side, shoved Spent aside and took the wheel. He backed onto the road and headed once again for Kunst's. His brother-in-law was not given to much belly laughing. Swag simply assumed that Spent was going through a crazy streak again.

The odd thing was that Werner Kunst counseled understanding. He talked about forgiveness. And he went off into a long rambling speech about last night's newspaper headlines, about the thinning of the earth's ozone layer. It had been confirmed again; apparently people in the tropics, especially white minorities, were dropping like flies from skin disease.

Kunst brought out a bottle of sunscreen lotion. "Got this just this morning, in the drugstore in Chesterton. Druggist says his supply was sold out an hour after the store opened. Says Blackout is the best seller. Says sunscreen lotion stock is way up on the market."

Kunst was preoccupied, made no move to sell drinks to Swag or Spent. "*Chicago Tribune* had an editorial on the whole thing today. Taking the hide off people yellin' about pollution control. The *Trib* says this economy can use every boost it can get, including sunscreen lotion sales. Small industry by itself. But things add up. They may be right. Kempt sees it that way. But I doubt those folks in the tropics do. Specially white men that moved down there to help the blacks make progress."

Swag whispered to Spent that Kunst had obviously been drinking. "Otherwise he would have given better advice on the dog."

Spent suggested that he and Swag buy a bottle and go home and tip up a few with Dorothy. They shook dice to see who would buy. Swag won.

CHAPTER 8

As often happens when calamity strikes, the depression that settled over Spent after the collapse of the rabbit-ranching scheme settled like a cold, noxious fog in the crevices and hollows of his ailments and fears. Migraines seemed to come more often. The flavors of his favorite whiskeys were flat. Commuters on the South Shore line seemed more cantankerous than ever. The news from Washington was gloomy, if not frightening. Not even Puffit's March nineteenth memorandum calling all faculty to an emergency meeting the next morning added much excitement.

The summit conference in Antarctica in which President Kempt and President Gassett of Chile were to agree on terms for establishment of the high-technology heat pump in Antarctica had ended in a public relations debacle. That whole affair had cast a pall on many Americans, including gung-ho futurists.

The crowds that swirled about the presidential limousine as Kempt disembarked from his helicopter after the flight from Tierra del Fuego had not been cheering, as early newscasts claimed, but jeering. In fact, they were intent on cornering both Kempt and the Chilean president in their limousines and incinerating them with gasoline bombs. It was only because of the quick thinking of Gassett's guards that the presidential parties escaped unharmed. The guards shot a half dozen of the mob and before the shock wore off the statesmen were stuffed back into their helicopters and flown away.

The mobs that attacked Presidents Kempt and Gassett had come swarming out of shanty towns that had sprung up all along the northern coast of Antarctica. The towns had grown up suddenly when krill harvesting boomed in the gelid southern waters. Mexican, Brazilian and Chilean fleets began massive seining operations in 1993 and they often anchored off the polar continental coast. Tired crews recreated in the sleazy cantinas and whorehouses that were the economic backbone of the bustling new communities.

It was apparent soon after krilling operations began that seining the small shrimplike creatures endangered the whale population that lived off them. Environmentalists, of course, cried out their indignation, noting that the whale would soon go the way of migratory birds and caribou. For a while their arguments seemed to prevail. But a United Nations Committee on the Immediate Abolition of Human Travail spoke out vigorously against "those who would subordinate human needs to those of the lower orders of creation." Political leaders of both the right and left seized upon the committee pronouncements as a way of easing the pressure of half-starved populations on them. They agreed that a logical application of the principles of reverence for life meant that they applied only to human beings. Albert Schweitzer, they noted, had not been a veterinarian.

A few strategic midnight arrests of the more vocal environmentalist troublemakers ended Latin American concern for the whale. Soon krilling operations were again fueling the population explosion from Mexico to Cape Horn. Now high-tech factory ships manufactured in Japan caught and ground up the krill. The oily slurry of protein was then shipped by rented Exxon tankers to Vera Cruz, Recife and Valparaiso. There it was dried and punched into cakes and distributed by truck and mule to ravenous Latins. But by 1996 the krill was gone, and the people of the polar shantytowns were immediately thrown back on a harsher life than ever.

The Third World was quick with advice again. The governments of Tanzania, Vietnam and Syria proposed a crash effort to assist the people of Antarctica to develop their land. Since tractors and gang plows were useless on the treeless, rocky continent they turned to Ireland for a new model of agricultural development. Pious, horny-fisted farmers were flown in from the island of Aran to demonstrate the use of seaweed in building tiny potato gardens amidst the stony, windswept barrens. Thereafter, day in and day out, from sunup to sundown and long after dark when a full moon allowed, the Chileans toiled. Back and forth like strange sleepless crabs, they lugged loads of soggy seaweed to their gardens. Each thousand pounds of seaweed reduced to a half ounce of humus. Barring high winds a family of five could build a ten-by-ten-foot garden in less than four years. But many died, emaciated as sticks from fatigue and scurvy, while the new game plan was being put in place. And so survivors, tight-jawed and harried, were in no mood for another grand plan from Washington or Santiago.

Most of the people who attacked the presidential limousines came from a town called Nuevo Francisco, so named to honor the man of Assisi's love of birds, as well as the memory of the Antarctic penguin.

Nuevo Franciscans had, of course, heard of the new American high-tech heat pump, the laser-pulse mass-driver system, LPMDS, that Kempt hoped to put in place to ventilate atmospheric heat through the hole that the magnetic pole formed in the Van Allen radiation belt. They had heard, too, that as soon as the system was operational they could follow their hearts' desire and migrate back to sooty factories in São Paulo, La Paz, and Caracas. But after the krill disappeared, as well as the money from big-spending krill-ship crews, they grew skeptical, even hostile toward anything from the outside. A new xenophobia, as sensitive and infectious as a boil, appeared.

So it was not difficult for a tiny, shrunken, half-starved Nuevo Franciscan widow to spread the rumor that the Americans were coming—with bulldozers. She had, she said, seen a yellow bulldozer deposited a week earlier from a huge, gray military aircraft at the nearby airstrip. Bulldozers meant one thing! The flattening of everything—mountains, hills, homes. She had seen bulldozers in her native village in Brazil, she said. There they razed the tropical forest of the Amazon as fast as the mowed-down areas could be blessed by priests for farms, even though the topsoil was thin and tropical rain tore it away in a few weeks. Bulldozers were demons, she insisted, as evil—perhaps more evil—than man. Bulldozers near Nuevo Francisco could only mean that the people's shantytown homes were to be flattened. The whole area would become a staging zone for the LPMDS project.

Her story of the bulldozer at the airport ricocheted like an outlaw bullet from one cantina to another, and there was still enough cheap mescal around to set red-eyed mobs swirling toward the airport, chanting "Down with LPMDS!" as the presidential helicopters came in to land.

The narrow escape of their president in Antarctica embittered many Americans, including commuters on Spent's trains. The whole wretched mess could only mean postponement of a high-tech solution to the greenhouse effect. So they grumbled and sweltered and cursed, venting their resentment or stroking their anxieties any way they could.

Some commuters displayed new fanatical zeal in attacking the crossword puzzles in their newspapers. Sitting on the old wicker seats of the South Shore, or on the wooden benches of the People Mover System's army trucks they slashed their way through one puzzle after another, scribbling angry graffiti in the margins whenever a word like *rhea, pampas* or *ice* came up.

But the rancor toward the Chileans that stirred the American heart showed itself to Spent in what appeared to him to be increasing numbers of just plain fools on the trains. They turned out in squads, platoons, brigades, it seemed, shoving, poking, exhaling, but always eating. They got on the trains with bags of potato chips, bags of cheeseburgers, candy bars, cheese curls, pretzels, apples, oranges (though fruit was now extremely expensive), tacos, enchiladas, coffee cake, sweet rolls, doughnuts, bagels, yogurt, sometimes a tomato, small pies, heavily frosted pieces of cake, fish sticks, and the latest wrinkles in postmodern junk food. They stuffed it into their mouths with both hands, chewed with their mouths open and drooled as they talked. It was against this backdrop of munching, swallowing, mouth-wiping and belching that the drama of urban life along the tracks unfolded for Spent.

The train always stopped at the far end of the Sixty-third Street dock, overlooking an enormous block of decaying tenements. On the second floor of the tenement building a rickety wooden porch still clung. Periodically a large black woman would emerge onto the porch dragging a small black boy of five or six. She would tie him to the porch railing, cut a switch from the spindly boxwood tree that reached up to the little porch and lash the boy mercilessly, then disappear with him back into the building. It was like some strange ritual to be performed only in the sun.

"Just like kids," said a munching specimen sitting next to Spent that Thursday toward the end of the month. A faint, embarrassed smile encircled a mouth full of hotdog, mustard and bun. "Always"—munch—"into something. Like my kid"—munch. "He's fighting with a magazine company"—swallow—"trying to collect on a money-back guarantee. It's a hobby journal. The kid sent"—munch—"for an instruction kit on how to make an old wheelbarrow handle into the stem for a hookah." Munch. "For smoking pot. Got the thing mixed up"—swallow. "Ruined it." Swallow, cough. "I tell him"—munch—"life is full of mistakes. I ask him, 'How do you think those scientists that predicted an ice age feel?' Take it easy, I tell him."

Spent stared straight ahead, then drew out his journal and began to make notes.

The muncher would have none of it. He leaned close.

"Damned prostate's acting up again. Takes me a half a day to take a leak. Ever see a picture of the prostate? It looks like a walnut."

Spent flinched.

"Know why they make so many mistakes in hospitals these days when they number urine samples? This heat. Nurses get irritable and deliberately interchange samples. My neighbor, name's Donovan, is supposed to have surgery. In the hospital a week . . . for tests. A nice man. Easy-going; easy to get along with. Got bladder surgery by mistake instead of removal of his larynx. How's that for the luck of the Irish?"

Another hotdog came out of the white paper bag.

"This is some story, isn't it?" Munch. A little finger pointed at the back side of Spent's newspaper. "This Porter County politician getting caught naked in his limo with a high school girl. Cop pulled over to help because of that low license plate number. This dummy tried to hide bare-assed in the cornfield near the road. But in that drought-stunted corn, he couldn't pull it off. Hiding, I mean. Had his clothes off already." Wipe. "Man. . ." Munch. "Look at this line—'Lawmaker indignant at press conference following arrest.' Calls for new gene splicing research at Indiana U. Wants to get corn to grow tall again. Top that?"

"I can't top that."

"Well, all the world's a stage." Munch. "Right?" An index finger went for a snag of onion, or perhaps gristle, between the first and second molar.

"Or a question of malocclusion," said Spent.

"Well a lot of people got that problem, that's for damn sure. Can be as bad as a swollen prostrate I suppose." Munch.

Spent slumped, ravaged, in his seat. His affliction left the train at the next stop.

Dean Thomas Alvin Puffit stood on the rostrum of the amphitheater of Timothy Leary Hall at FSU. "First the bad news," he began. "Our educational delivery system has been destroyed."

A gasp, followed by a low groan, rose from the assembled faculty.

Puffit told the story in short, intense bursts. "Burglars broke into the audio-visual equipment room between two and three in the morning. A smashed clock reads two-thirty. Trashed everything—projectors, speakers, recorders, film, amplifying equipment. The whole thing hammered, battered, burnt. Smoke from the film set off the alarms."

"Oh, my God!" moaned an educator to the left.

"Terrorism!" shouted someone in the middle of the room.

Puffit was seated at a small table on the rostrum. He stared down at the table for a moment. His eyes rose slowly, then swept across the room. For a moment, Spent felt they had settled on him.

"We are, indeed," said Puffit in a cold, dispassionate voice, "victims of a new terrorism. We are witnessing the willful, vicious destruction of everything, and anything, that is born of high technology. During the seventies and eighties, terrorist groups around the world took hostages, blew up aircraft, bombed banks. But *never* anything like this. A deadly perversion has become the mark of this postmodern terrorism."

"Lynch the bastards!" shouted someone from the back.

"That's the bottom line!" Puffit shouted in return. "And many others across this great land of ours interface with the same bottom line impacting the problem—nation-wise."

"Time to dust off the death penalty," called out a tall, thin, graying professor who'd made his way to the front of the room.

Spent remembered the fellow. He was the target of the Koffee Klatch waitress's withering blast, "Eat your fruit, fruit!" Apparently he had made a full recovery.

Puffit, now on his feet also, waved a two-foot-square sheet of brown paper. The crude figure drawn on it could have been a broken spinning wheel or a small, rampant monkey with its tail cut off. "This grotesque thing is their symbol! It was nailed to the storeroom door!"

The professor, still standing, hissed.

Puffit acknowledged the contribution, then began again. "We are not the only targets of this senseless violence."

"Tell him about Zion!" shouted the professor, now seated.

"They're gathering strength at this very moment to stop progress at that power plant," responded the dean. "Neo-Luddites, they're called. Read the papers. It was on the front page this morning, up front."

A wave of hisses, curses, and "Fuck 'em alls!" washed across the room as the educators vented their fury.

"They're fighting entombment! That gives you an idea of what we're up against," shouted Puffit, confident that his faculty was now in his pocket.

More hisses, followed by a variety of scatological formulations.

The "entombment" to which Puffit referred was an announcement earlier in the year of government plans to terminate operation of the Zion atomic power plant north of Chicago. The plant had been in use since the early sixties and was nearing its decommission deadline. It was to be pumped full of concrete and abandoned.

But the media discovered reports published in *Science* back in 1982 that physicists had found radioactive nickel among the residues infesting aged reactors. Nickel 59 has a half-life of eighty thousand years, which is seventy-five thousand years more than the concrete that was supposed to entomb it. The report splattered planners like a rock hitting a mud puddle. Plans for boldly recycling atomic industry blunders abruptly lost their grip on the imagination. Kempt's secretary of the interior, riding the crest of popularity that followed establishment of the Moonscape Wonder Parks, had proposed to use decommissioned atomic reactors in a kind of high-tech Appian Way stretching across the country. Entombed reactors were to be connected with a colorful roadway signage system and hyped over television as the "Highway of the Twentieth Century." Each tomb was to be named after a great inventor in the American technological saga, Whitney, Bell, McCormick, Fermi, and the like. The new "tomb park system" was to be brought on line during the Year 2000 celebrations.

Environmentalists attacked the highway scheme as soon as the secretary's announcement was made. They insisted that future tourists, including mothers with babes in arms, would be radiated by nickel 59 long after the secretary was out of office. In fact, long after secretaries of the interior, in general, were dead and gone.

Physicists agreed with the environmentalists. They demonstrated that extinct atomic power plants would have to be cut up by heavy remote control equipment and buried in massive vaults cut into pre-Cambrian rock deposits in northern Michigan and Wisconsin. They said, too, that chopping up the tiny Elk River reactor in Minnesota back in the seventies cost $6.15 million and took two years of painstaking work. The cost of demolishing and burying the big reactors as they were decommissioned would dwarf the Elk River budget.

"But enough of this Zion business," said Puffit. "Need I tell you what the assault on our audio-visual delivery system means? Need I ask what this senseless violence means?"

An angry voice erupted near the rear of the room. "Where the fuck was our security?"

Puffit ignored the shout. "This destruction of our delivery system means we shall have to fall back on every sort of anachronism. It means using books! It means forcing students to read! It means forcing them to write!"

A female teacher in the front row of the amphitheater began to weep softly, her shoulders hunched, shuddering.

Puffit looked down at the stricken educator. "My dear," he said, "I share your grief and your outrage."

The angry voice near the rear would not be consoled. "Where the *fuck* was our security?"

The dean continued, ignoring his detractor. "For those of you who have built your classroom delivery systems around the discussion mode, things will not be critical immediately. But we have all used audio-visuals as our means for staying abreast. It *is*, after all, the state of the art. We have all grown to know and love such classics as 'Understanding Your Sexual Preference Compulsion,' not to mention that fine classic, 'Adventuring in Chemical Dependence.'"

"Horse manure!" shouted the hostile voice from the rear. "Where the hell was our security!?"

The tide began to turn against Puffit when someone else bellowed out, "You're in trouble, Puffit!"

The dean, annoyed and intimidated, motioned impatiently to a portly man in dark gray overalls sitting in the front row to come to the microphone. He was a night watchman and sometime janitor. He would address the group, said the dean, concerning locks.

The night watchman moved slowly to the microphone. He surveyed the audience as gravely as Churchill speaking to British citizenry after a Nazi aerial onslaught. He told the faculty everything he knew about locks. He described lever tumbler locks, pin tumbler locks, deadbolt locks, locks that do one thing, locks that do another, and finally a new lock coming off the assembly line in Detroit at Dork Lock Incorporated. The Dork lock was made of compressed sawdust, with Elmer's glue as the bonding agent. It was an ingenious device, the watchman allowed, given the shortage of metals like tungsten. Its major drawback was that it tended to melt into a gooey lump if exposed to moisture.

The watchman, enjoying the role of commentator on the times, turned philosophic. "Folks," he said, "I never seen a lock that couldn't be broke or picked. Never! And I been in this work for many years. But that ain't as bad as some people think. What would be the result if someone invented a foolproof lock? Think about it! What would be the result, the consequences, as you educated people might say? The end to improvement in locks! Then and there. No more progress in makin' locks! Bang. The end!" He thumped his fist into his hand. "It's somethin' that some of you may forget in things like this. So don't go round lookin' for perfect answers. If it wasn't for a break-in now and then, industries like Dork would have to shut their doors. 'Course, I see things different—from the blue-collar side. I'm a plain man, even though I know a thing or two. Thank you."

Puffit beamed.

The faculty was no less impressed with the watchman. He had laid the axe to the root. His was the kind of no-nonsense talk that the FSU faculty understood and honored. Applause engulfed him as he returned to his seat.

The dean immediately seized on the upbeat mood the watchman had created. "Folks," he said as the applause died down, "now the good news! The dragnet is out for the vicious animals that wrecked the A-V delivery system. The police are already working hard on it. They have assigned Lieutenant Kastowitz—this gentleman sitting here in the front row—to the job. Would you stand please, lieutenant?"

Kastowitz, a small man with a tree-shrew face, stood. He was dressed in a trench coat, and sweat ran down his cheeks. He bowed to the applauding faculty and sat down.

Puffit, waving his arms over his head like a victorious prize fighter, adjourned the meeting.

On his way to the train that day, Spent didn't stop at The Heist. Instead, he ducked into a small stand-up bar in the terminal, Gracie's Pit Stop, and smoothed down three or four Wild Turkeys.

There was a police car in the Swagmacher driveway when he got home that evening. He took a deep breath and went inside. Dorothy greeted him with an embrace. He tousled Timmy's hair as the boy bolted through the door to join his brother Kenny in a game of Cops and

Robbers, the police car in the yard a fortuitous prop.

Dorothy introduced the Indiana State Patrol officers. They were seated in the kitchen over cups of coffee. Both were immaculately uniformed in deep blue with gold trim, set off with enormous shoulder patches, braids and whistle lanyards.

The senior officer, a sergeant, was a squat, dark fellow named Kearn. The other was a blond young man of about twenty; trim, very polite, hazel-eyed, something from a TV screen.

Kearn did most of the talking. "Mr. Spent, we're told you have developed some new concepts in police work. A transom unit measure for screening suspects. It's called 'TUM,' I understand. What's the basic idea of the thing?"

Spent went through the essentials of TUM as he had for Puffit back in February, questions of length and width of transoms, the need for doing cross sectional calculations on the size of suspects and his special caveat on the use of TUM with suspects trained in yoga.

Kearn listened intently, hunkered down under a heavy frown. "You take considerable interest in this whole idea of breaking and entering, I take it?"

Spent responded with a smile bathed in the afterglow of Gracie's Pit Stop. "To understand breaking and entering is to understand the human heart."

The sergeant shook his head as if trying to come awake. "Well... and what time did you return home the night before last? The night of the storeroom break-in at FSU?"

"He was home early, sergeant. I remember that. Home around seven," Dorothy interjected.

The sergeant's eyebrows fused over his massive brow ridge. The brow ridge of a race tinctured by leftover genes from Neanderthal man, thought Spent.

"I returned at eventide, to the sound of barking dogs," Spent said playfully. "With Emily Dickinson I put the sunset in a cup. On the rocks."

"Did you visit the audio-visual storeroom the day before yesterday in connection with your work? We understand you do audio-visual setups for the senior faculty. You're one of the few who have keys to that room. Correct?"

"Yes. I have keys to Puffit's kingdom, sergeant. Keys, keys and more keys." He pulled out a ring of keys and jiggled them. "Rather nice tone, don't you think?"

Kearn was not amused. "Did you return to the storeroom on the night in question?"

"To those who know the meaning of the day, all nights are equally in question."

"Mr. Spent, we know from your sister that you are a philosopher. But nonetheless, could you please answer questions forthrightly. Did you or did you not break into the storeroom or help others do it?"

"Sergeant, direct questions are all too often evidence of indirect intentions. Perhaps you could phrase your query with just a touch of grace?"

The cop bristled. "We are not here to pray. We're here to find out who wrecked that equipment. And we know about that underground Ludder group."

"Luddite."

"Stick to the question."

"Your question is sensible enough, considering what Emily once said of open doors: 'Ajar-inviting.' It never did betray the soul that asked its shelter in solemn honesty."

Kearn's partner looked at the ceiling. "Off his twig, Bill. Better give it up."

Dorothy Swagmacher interrupted. "Please, Cass. Talk nice to the officers. They're only doing their jobs, you know. And forget this Emily. I thought it was Violet you loved."

Kearn turned to Dorothy. "Mrs. Swagmacher," he said,

"if this Emily was an accessory, she'll have her own explaining to do."

Spent said, "I am sure humankind would agree with that. For she once said that 'even a careless word can breed infection'."

Kearn stood. "Well, suit yourself, Spent. We're taking you in for questioning. Maybe a week in the slammer will clear your head."

Dorothy's face grew ashen. She turned her face away, stifling a gasp. There were tears in her eyes. "Please, officer," she said, "can I talk to my brother privately before you leave?"

Kearn grunted his approval, then motioned his partner to cover the exit from the kitchen. He walked into the living room.

"For God's sake, Cass!" she whispered heatedly, "why did you have to talk that way to *these* men? You're usually so unafraid. But they think you're off your rocker! You'll end up in the asylum down at Valpo. They won't keep you in jail. They'll put you in the nuthouse. And you've had a few drinks, I can tell! I know you keep that CC in your room. You ought to stick to beer, like Swag. I mean Cass, you really..."

The sergeant interrupted. "Okay, folks. We're taking Mr. Spent in now. You can visit him in the jug." He patted Dorothy's arm. "Frankly ma'am, I think your brother may be sick, very sick," he said. "We see a lot of them. The heat don't help much."

A half hour later, Spent was turned over to Illinois authorities at the tollway border stop. An hour after that, he was booked, fingerprinted, shoved into a squad car and taken to Cook County jail. There he was shoved into a cell occupied by a dozen assorted felons, pimps and drunks.

"What you in here for?" asked a small, black, intense-looking youngster of seventeen or eighteen.

"Don't know." Spent was tired. He slumped to the floor at one end of the cell. "Don't know, but it's got something to do with my higher education."

"What do you do for a livin' man, I mean?" the teenager persisted, squatting next to Spent. "Them clothes of yours is okay. You don't look busted." He grinned at Spent. "You don't look like you're really with it either, man."

"I'm a professor of philosophy. FSU," said Spent.

"Holy blue balls on a Christmas tree!" shouted the black kid. "Hey, you guys! Come and get this one. We got a philosopher here. A prof. A *real* one."

"Frost my nuts and call me Santa Claus," said another. "Now we gonna find out what is truth and what is reality."

The prisoners drew around Spent. There was genuine admiration on the faces of all of them. They began pressing Spent for answers, answers to everything.

"The thing I want to know, Socrates," said one, "is how in hell a man can relax in this fuckin' heat? This hole has gotta be one hundred and ten degrees!"

"In the shade," shouted another.

"What is shade?" another asked.

"It ain't reality, that's for goddamn sure," someone else said. "Not since those assholes screwed up the climate, it ain't."

The questions flew back and forth for almost an hour. Spent scarcely said a word. Then abruptly all but two of the prisoners were taken out of the cell. The seminar came to an end.

Spent napped off and on through the night. In the morning he and the other two prisoners were served breakfast, a kind of gruel made of ground Canadian wheat and powdered milk whipped to a froth.

That afternoon Spent was allowed to visit briefly with Dorothy and Swag. Dorothy babbled something about the jailers, saying that they seemed both kind and unafraid. Then they were asked to leave.

Abruptly, with some cursing and shoving, the two other prisoners were removed from the cell. Spent was alone. For hours he heard nothing but the clang of cell doors along the corridor.

Then lunch was served. It was another bowl of gruel, topped off with what might have been dried pears. The guard served it mechanically. "The boys tell me you're a philosopher," he said as he slid the bowl on a tray through an opening at the bottom of the door. "I got a kid that's into that too. Reads Romans. Says we're all ready to cut our wrists in a bathtub full of warm water. Make it cold water and I'll join him."

The guard shoved a rolled-up page of the morning paper into the cell. "Only one page, but it'll keep ya busy. Takes me all morning to get through one of them pages."

His lunch finished, Spent unrolled the newspaper page, stroked it flat on the musty mattress of the cell bunk and began to savor it. One side was entirely ads for a new "Water Miser" washing machine, guaranteed to get by on a gallon of water a week. The other side of the page was part of the arts and leisure section. There were two reviews of paintings, one about an auction of a cache of erotica attributed to Norman Rockwell, the other about efforts of Chicago area art patrons to have three large auto junkyards near Skokie designated historical preservation sites. Junk scavengers across the country had reduced most of the giant yards, once a favorite haunt of sculptors, to a pathetic handful. There was also a theater review. A new play had opened at the Strasberg Theater on Congress Avenue. It apparently was a hit, now in its second week. Somehow, perhaps because of the excitement of dating Violet, perhaps of being fired, Spent had missed it. William Richelieu reviewed it:

> *Midnight and the Gastropod* is the story of a South Mollucan brother and sister. It is the story of their struggle toward full sexual identity as incestuous lovers, their shatteringly honest preference.
>
> Mr. Karmel brings home the torment of their adolescent predicament by subtle devices reminiscent of Beckett. There are two long scenes of total silence in which the lovers stand nude, merely touching fingers, or exploring their sexuality with poignant curiosity, as they watch, compulsively, one guesses (though this is never certain), the hermaphroditic coupling of a pair of snails in the household tropical fish tank.
>
> The playwright's statement is brilliant, using every skill for which he is so justly famous. Torn between the demands of Mollucan freedom-fighters to join in a suicidal foray against Indonesian tyrants and the deep, abiding, all-too-human need to stay at home and stare at snails, the characters deliver their lines sparingly but with enormous power, displaying the mastery of theatrical counterpoint that is Mr. Karmel's special gift.
>
> The boy (Willard Horn) and the girl (Jean Box) are placed in the home of a wealthy Mollucan merchant, a smuggler of sweet potatoes and tail feathers of the extinct bird of paradise. But they are also members of a secret Marxist coven that meets in the cellar of the abandoned wing of the family mansion.
>
> I cannot say more without saying too much. This is Karmel at his finest, and Horn and Box at their very, very best. This play is a must for 1997. It is destined to become a classic of the terribly insightful tradition. Oooo, Oooo, the Karmel oeuvre! Need I say more?

Now that the Kowalski look had hit Chicago, thanks largely to the stylish Mr. Richelieu, theatergoing had taken on a whole new dimension. Spent knew that Violet Fromel would love to undress for the theater. And he could take another run at this whole postmodern thing.

Spent vowed to take Violet to the play as soon as he got out of jail. It would be a way to get close enough to her to unburden his heart on the fate of the hasenpfeffer scheme.

CHAPTER 9

Tom Puffit sat in his undershirt, the new red, white and blue BVD cut, at his large glass-and-steel desk squinting at a packet of material ferried to him from Spent's cell in Cook County jail. His right arm was in a sling and there was a blue-black welt on his cheekbone an inch or so from one eye. He muttered small, impatient curses and epithets as he fingered the documents.

"Shit. Screw. This goddamn crap."

Jenny Perch hovered near his desk with a bucket of ice cubes. "Perhaps a cold pack on that elbow would help, dean?"

"To hell with ice packs, Jen," he said grimacing. "That ice belongs in my bourbon. Bourbon's the only thing that'll remove the pain in my ass that Spent put there."

Perch said nothing. Puffit was cranky. He had to be handled with kid gloves.

"The bastard's a real threat. Even from jail. *He* set those goons on me, whether the cops think so or not. Well, there's more than one way to skin a cat. I had Lieutenant Kastowitz spring the sonofabitch this morning. You send

Roscoe over with the limo to pick him up as I instructed?"

"Yes, dean."

"Good. Kastowitz is joining us here in twenty minutes. When Spent shows up, we treat him like he's a big shot. We'll have a drink here and then go to the faculty lounge for a come-as-you-are party. Might as well kill two birds with one stone. The damn party was scheduled anyway and Spent will be flattered to be asked to join senior faculty. Kastowitz says if we can get a half dozen drinks into the maniac he'll start talking. Kastowitz bugged a few chairs and the table where we put out the booze. We'll find out where that bastard is coming from."

"I thought he was coming from jail, dean."

"It's a manner of speaking! For God's sake. Now let me read this shit."

"Just trying a little humor, dean."

Puffit flushed, then apologized. "Sorry. It's this damn elbow. Stick around."

There were two documents on the desk in front of Puffit. One was a drawing by Spent, on wrapping paper of some kind. The other was a Spent memo, a long one from what Puffit could tell. It was written, sort of printed, on the inside of three business envelopes torn open and pressed flat.

"Look at this, Jen, and tell me this guy isn't off his rocker." He shoved the drawing across his desk. "He's got Jesus dragging around a cross with a wheel on it. And down below he's got this caption, 'High-tech comes to the Via Dolorosa.' And this crown of thorns? A note here says it's made out of 'postindustrial watercress.' He can be a snide bastard, I'll give him that."

Perch was bewildered.

"Toss off a drink yourself, Jen. Glasses over there in the cabinet. This goddamned memo is worse than the drawing. Besides, look at the length of it! The man's a bully.

Nobody with a civilized bone in his body would make a person read something this long."

Perch quickly poured a drink and downed it, twisting her face.

"Use some water, for Christ's sake, Jen," Puffit said gruffly. "More bourbon where that came from."

Perch grinned and freshened her drink. She knew Puffit was on the make; had been, in fact, since the day he hired her. But his squat, shoulderless body put her off. And he was almost fifty-five. The fact that his hair was almost gone didn't help either. She liked burly, curly-haired, sweaty-looking men, the kind with natural body odor. She did not go for the new synthetic, spray-on sweat odors, the pheremones that cosmetic companies were pushing so hard on TV. The pheremones always reminded her of the smell of a Sears tire service center. Puffit used the pheremones, to be sure, being a dean and a high-tech devotee, but to Perch he came off smelling like a four-ply retread rather than the real thing.

Besides, there were plenty of naturally smelly brutes in the student body. And Perch made the most of it, or at least so the gossip said.

In any case, laying pipe with Perch was still one of the little delectations that had eluded Puffit. But it remained at the back of his mind always and when he was with Perch it produced a strange mixture of strutting, boasting, whining and indecision.

"Sit down and listen to some of this, Jen." He began to read Spent's memo to her:

May 6, 1997

To: Thomas Alvin Puffit, Dean
The School of Education, FSU

From: Casper Martin Spent
Assistant Professor, FSU

RE: Insult

Though I sit in this cage and age like cheddar, I would remind you that the messenger of truth often disguises itself as insult.

Begin at the beginning! When we were extruded into this world, to the sound of our mother's groans, the truth of our sudden predicament was gore-smeared, bruised and cold. We glimpsed the world—stainless steel and chrome, glaring like a butcher's knife under a thousand fluorescent lights—through eyelids puffed and pink and tender as an albino salamander's. We were like some shivering marsupial banished forever from its fur-fringed home. We were helpless as grubs upon a stone. But we knew God.

"How sweet," Jenny sighed.

"Come on," said Puffit. "Humans are as helpless as grubs on a stone? The man is a goddamn menace any way you slice it."

Jenny frowned. "Slicing a menace" posed for her a brief conceptual problem.

Puffit rose from his desk, wandered to the window, the memo held awkwardly in his right hand, the drink in his left. He sipped the bourbon.

"That all he wrote, dean?"

"Wish it was. This damn thing goes on and *on*. Get this."

Lying on our mother's belly we wailed our larval helplessness and tried to read the future in her pain-weary eyes. Alas, Tom, the eyes are mirrors! And the mirror is the cruelest invention of them all. True, the wheel is a great invention. But at best it can only teach us the meaning of repetition. But the mirror! What a tireless silver shuttle, forever iterating vanity, as terrible in its beauty as Eve's lust for the winesaps of Eden.

"That's really quite beautiful," Jenny said. "What does it mean?"

"Oh, it's some damn play on Old Testament applesauce. Spent's a philosophy type, don't forget. Thinks the wheel and the mirror started all our troubles. Well, personally, I *like* wheels and I *like* mirrors. I'm an optimist, Jen. Spent hates that in me. But remember one thing. Philosophy and optimism don't mix. Never did. Never will." Puffit winced as he lifted his arm and resettled it in his sling. "Let things go sour a bit, like this weather thing, and those yoyos come out of the woodwork like cockroaches."

"Are you going to read some more?"

Puffit frowned. He was annoyed with Perch's reaction to the memo. She liked the damn thing. She never was too bright, he told himself. Stupid, in fact. But a superb screw, he'd heard, and God, how he would love to dip the wick, just once. He continued reading:

> Insult assures attention. Consider what attention did for wit! In the 1890s horses pulled trams along the streets of our great cities. By 1900 there were 150,000 in New York City alone. Lashed, for sake of progress, until their nostrils bled, they each produced twenty pounds of manure a day. That is a half billion pounds of manure to welcome each equinox.

Perch sat motionless, enthralled. "It's the big words that get to me, dean," she explained, "and the grand ideas. We don't hear those much around here. We get 'in' words, of course, and lots of honesty. I know we live in an age of honesty. The paper said so again, just this morning."

Puffit bridled. "Don't forget, Jen, men who can't do a damn thing with their lives always fall back on words."

Perch stared at him. There was a hurt look on her face.

Puffit shrugged, said "Shit!" under his breath and read on:

May I remind you of the invention of chewing gum? It was not enough for our forefathers to run about the woods chewing spruce pitch, as they did in Boone's day, spitting proudly each time they discharged their muskets at presuming Indians. Now we have gum made of polyethylene, plyvinyl, massanranduba balata, not to mention gutta hang kang.

The *Wall Street Journal* tells us that the Metro Authority scrapes, each day, from seats, floors, walls and ceilings of that great city's subway system 1,149,000 wads of gum. Does this insult serve no other end than to instigate the hype, to cause the advertiser to levitate in his sleep?

"Got enough?" asked Puffit.

"No," Perch said without hesitation.

Resigned, his voice sarcastic, Puffit read the rest of the memo:

I end with this. I know every foot of the commuter line as it passes beyond Gary to my home. I know the ramshackle houses near the tracks. I know the backyard with the rotting picket fence and the dog pen. I know the captive timber wolf chained there. Last week, from the windows of the stalled train, I read this message in its yellow eyes:

On the long chain of human crime
It is tied about your neck as surely as this hateful collar
The chain rusts slowly and mildew grays the leather
I twist and ache in a world grown hideous as a tumor

I have survived the red hot bullet and forest fire
Now the brook and the pine are scorched and dry
The wilderness I roam is a patch of dirty rags alive with vermin
And in the heavens only a soiled moon survives

God has taught the wolf and the centipede
To hunt with the power and skill of Orion

Soon the human race will sicken and falter
What I cannot kill, the centipede will sting and then devour.

Spent's memorandum was signed as usual, with the unicorn and his initials.

"Well, that's it," Puffit said triumphantly, as if he had survived an ordeal. He was sure he had.

Jenny Perch stared out the window. Spent's discourse on mirrors, horses bleeding through the nostrils, chewing gum, God and the wolf had left her stunned. She had never thought much about progress before.

The ringing of the telephone broke the spell. Spent would be downstairs in a few minutes.

The limousine driver held the door open as Spent alighted in front of Freedom State's administration building. He was still in his striped prison fatigues, his dress clothes wrapped in a bundle of newspaper under one arm.

Puffit met Spent at the revolving door at the entrance to the building.

"My God, Cass, that was a real mistake, throwing you into the slammer. What can I say, except to apologize for some fool mistake by the police?" He took Spent's arm and hurried him onto the elevator and up to the dean's suite on the tenth floor.

Spent was surprised by Puffit's battered appearance, but he made no comment on it. He was all business. "I presume you got my memorandum?"

"Of course I did. Splendid. Excellent. Clear and concise and to the point, as usual." They entered the dean's office. Puffit showed Spent to one of the large lounge chairs at one end of his office. "Now, sit down, Cass. We can have a cool one."

Spent sat, said nothing.

"And what would you like, Cass?" asked Puffit. "By

way of a pick-me-up? I have gin, whiskey—your favorite, I believe, Wild Turkey?" He hovered near a small liquor cabinet to one side of his chair. "Perhaps a hit of grass with your drink? Or a snort of coke? I have some excellent support systems."

"Turkey will do," said Spent.

"Good. Excellent. Fine drink, Turkey." Puffit rambled on about this and that as he fixed drinks, then took a chair. "Lieutenant Kastowitz of the Chicago Police Department will join us here. The man I introduced to the faculty a few days ago after the trashing of our delivery system. I'm sure you remember him. Then we'll go to the faculty lounge for a few drinks and snacks. Senior faculty affair. Nothing big, of course—although we are celebrating a new OUSTIF grant. Informal, a come-as-you-are sort of thing." He eyed Spent's prison fatigues. "Didn't know they used that stripe anymore. But it's become a classic, I suppose."

Spent sipped his drink. "Hot. The weather, not my drink," he said.

"Yes, a bit warm. Been going about without my shirt most of the day. Temperature hit one hundred and five at one o'clock. But a front went through. It's down to ninety-eight. Cooling trend. Part of the turnaround, I'm sure. Heat wave's bottomed out."

"So I'm told. Guards at Cook County said they saw the announcement on TV."

"Reassuring, right, Cass?"

"About as reassuring as we can expect, Tom."

Perch showed Kastowitz in. The lieutenant was in his trench coat, insisting that he keep it on. His grayish eyebrows pinched down over his narrow, shrew face as he eyed Spent during the introductions.

Puffit tossed off a joke about the man who loved heat so much he found heaven a bore. The joke fell flat. Then he said to Kastowitz, "Spent here is a creative fellow. Writer, artist. Very gifted with the sketch pad. Ask him to do your portrait some time, lieutenant."

"I'll do it now," said Spent.

"Now?" Puffit asked.

"The present is all we have, Tom. That's why we don't need to worry about the future. Isn't that in the Freedom State alma mater?"

Puffit could feel his anger building. Spent was playing games again. As a futurist, "now" thinking always left Puffit feeling a bit unsteady. He liked "now" thinking, enjoyed every moment of it, in fact. But life got complicated when tenses got scrambled. True, to a good futurist, the future is now. Now wasn't the future, of course. Or was it? A light-headed feeling came over Puffit. Tension, perhaps. The mere presence of Spent.

The lieutenant, as decisive a man of his time as the next person, sensed Puffit's uncertainty. He positioned himself in his chair in partial profile, flipping the collar of his trench coat up. He placed one hand on his knee and froze.

Spent walked boldly to Puffit's desk, picked up the desk blotter pad, turned it over. "There comes a tide in every man's life," he said, "including cops." He began sketching Kastowitz on the back of the pad.

"Well," Puffit sputtered, taken aback by the odd little scene before him. "I'm not sure we should be creative during office hours."

Spent returned the blotter pad to the desk without smiling.

The cop remained frozen in his pose. Puffit cleared his throat, went over to Kastowitz and gently touched his shoulder. "Time to go, lieutenant."

Kastowitz blinked. "Of course. Time to go." The three of them left for the party in the faculty lounge.

* * *

Spent could tell from the swiveling heads of the thirty or more faculty who were in the lounge hovering about the table of hors d'oeuvres and liquor bottles that his stint in the cooler had made him something of a celebrity. He felt pleased with himself.

It was a rather typical faculty reception. The precious, the precocious and the quietly disturbed swirled about in chattering little clusters of three and four, misinterpreting one another's comments with happy abandon. Words like "outrageous," "irrepressible" and "incorrigible" skittered and ping-ponged about the room.

One cluster of faculty was admiring the latest FSU fine arts acquisition near the west wall of the lounge. It was a floor-to-ceiling, thirty-foot-long series of green-tinted photographs, all eight inches square and identical. They were pictures of a lump of stool with a demitasse spoon stuck into it. It was entitled *Compulsion Turd 500*. The debate of the educators concerned whether the work was irrepressible or incorrigible. All agreed it was not really outrageous.

Another cluster of faculty members was excitedly discussing wines and food. One, a crew-cut young woman dressed in leather shorts and bra, resolute and bellicose as a cowhand, dominated. She extolled a dingy restaurant in Lisbon where the house wine cost fifteen cents a bottle and the menu favorite was an almost extinct octopus garnished with moss from the bark of a nearly extinct Pyrénées evergreen.

That discussion moved on to bloodless bullfights. The sober observation of an elderly professor was that they were obviously the moral equivalent of gore.

"Cass! You outrageous old swashbuckler! Sit down." It was Anselm Pester. He was sitting, or lying, in a sort of heap across one of the lounge chairs. He was shirtless, in tattered denim shorts with the fly deliberately left open; a touch of fashion that had replaced the unbuttoned shirt of the seventies and eighties, and Third World pumps of a kind Spent had not seen before, a crushed Coca-Cola can arching across each instep. He yanked Spent down into one of the chairs.

"Why did you wait for this historic moment, getting thrown into the slammer, I mean? I understand there was a riot there last month when the warden was caught black-marketing electric fans to his back-cell friends. Three or four cons killed. Could have lost you. We need you around here to run errands."

"I'm a better-late-than-never bloomer, Anselm," said Spent, gulping the remainder of his whiskey as he tried to seat himself.

But Spent did not stay in the chair long before Puffit came looking for him. "There you are, Cass," he said. "Come along now. Move about a bit. You're the guest of honor, you know."

Perch was with Puffit. "You know Jenny, of course. She thinks you're quite the thinker, Cass. Loved your memorandum."

Perch blushed. She remembered her "Don't go limp in the heat" remark to Spent a month or so ago in the cafeteria. As if to apologize, she said, "One of the most beautiful and virile things I have ever heard, professor."

Spent let his eyes circle carelessly about the room, then settle on the bridge of Perch's nose. He knew she had intellectual pretensions, primitive and undeveloped though they were. He said slowly, "Beauty is a subject to which I have given some thought and some pen."

"Understanding it is so difficult sometimes," said Perch.

"A journey of a thousand miles begins with one step," said Spent, holding back.

Pester horned in. "Bullshit, man! Not the kind of trip this party needs." He pulled out a small packet that resembled a coin purse, fished inside, then pulled out a colorful little pill. He tossed it into his mouth and washed it down with his drink.

"You write with such style, professor," said Perch, ignoring Pester.

"Truth can reveal itself in style," said Spent loftily.

"Crap," said Pester, now on the fringes of the conversation.

Puffit tried to get two cents worth in. "I'm sure the truth lies somewhere..."

Perch cut in. "That's why he's trying to find it."

"Style is the hand engraving on the invitation sent us by Fate to attend an execution, to attend the great, cosmic hanging we call life," said Spent, not making much sense.

Perch sighed. "Very philosophical."

"Speaking of hangings..." Puffit began.

"Let him go at it, for Pete's sake," Perch said impatiently.

"Speaking of hangings..." Puffit began again.

"Please talk more, Professor Spent," said Perch. Her eyes sparkled as she listened to the conversation. And whenever Puffit tried to say something she would put her hand up and shush him with a "Please..."

Spent let out sail. He felt himself running with a strong following wind. "Man needs more than the feel of the meatball of common sense in his belly. He needs the meringue of intellectual reflection as well."

"Polka-dot bullshit!" said Pester, his pupils dilated.

"Wish I understood those words," said Perch. "Not yours, Mr. Pester, his." She smiled at Spent.

"He's off his nut," said Pester, staring about the room, scratching his chest and stomach, insouciant as a barbarian fart.

Spent let out spinnaker. "Be of good cheer, my friends.

As I have said in one of my essays, 'Hooves, mane, nostrils, blowhole, everything about God and love and pain is already known to those who pay attention. We must face it all in faith, faith in everything, including analgesics.'"

"I heard that word," shrieked Perch delightedly. "On television. It's aspirin!"

"Sure it ain't something for the crabs?" Pester said disdainfully.

"Really, Anselm!" said Puffit, trying to let Perch know he thought she was a lady and ought to be treated as such, which of course he did not. He wanted to get into her pants, nothing more, nothing less. "Just because Jen doesn't know..."

Spent looked at the dean, the patience of a thousand years in his eyes. "I quote the noble Lao Tsu," he said.

> By continual losing
> One reaches doing nothing.
> By doing nothing everything is done.

Puffit was exasperated. "More of your goddamned no-growth talk." The party began to wind down.

As far as Puffit and Kastowitz were concerned the party had been a flop. Kastowitz had returned to Puffit's office just before the bar shut down and played the tapes the receiver system he had been carting about under his trench coat had picked up from the bugs. When he returned to the reception he told Puffit they seemed useless. All that had happened was that Spent had paraded himself about like a goddamned mad genius and Perch had found him irresistible.

The whole thing galled Puffit. He downed three more drinks and careened back to his office on Pester's arm.

Pester was giggling. He intended to make hay while the sun shone.

Kastowitz, too, felt let down. He grumped about the lounge in his trench coat, grousing at the bald, ocher-smeared coed tending bar. "We ran out of hors d'oeuvres, for Chrissake!"

On the train, Spent's prison garb drew no attention from the commuters other than a wink from a pimply faced teenage girl and a comment, "You look cute as a bug in that thing, mister. That the latest out east?"

Everyone else was wrapped up in his or her own sultry little world, doing crossword puzzles, dozing or bitching about the latest news from Washington. Someone out there had come up with another scheme for cooling things down. It called for installation of giant pumps in the deep trenches of the Atlantic and Pacific to force the cold benthic currents to the surface where they would soak up some of the atmosphere's heat. A half dozen giant transnational engineering firms had, in fact, been awarded big grants for pilot research. Then a young, upstart oceanographer asked, in a letter to the editor of the *Washington Post,* what was to be done to get the warm water down to the sea floor again so that it could cool. And when he was asked to appear before Senate hearings on Operation Upwelling, he asked the same question again. The mortified project planners had no answer. They left the hearings to the sound of catcalls and hisses.

Even the chairman of the committee, himself an avid supporter of the 'High Tech Now' coalition that had formed to fight environmentalists, was chagrined. "Didn't those dumb bunnies know heat rises? They should have amended a law of physics or *some* damn thing. We amend laws around here all the time."

When Spent got home he did not waste any time reading the evening paper as he usually did. He joined Swag and Dorothy briefly on the porch for a few beers. They were listening to the whirring of cicadas in the trees behind the house. Then Spent took a shower, fixed himself a snack and went to his room. He put his mind to his new agenda.

CHAPTER 10

Like most FSU students, the two who showed up at Spent's office the morning after the faculty reception were blotched with acne. Although acne therapy had made giant strides in the early eighties, it suffered a severe setback in 1993 when a variant form of amebiasis entered the country via Canary Island homosexuals. It was then spliced with a remnant exotic strain of acne staphylococcus kept at a Salt Lake City laboratory for military research purposes. A CIA officer had come up with the idea of crossing the two organisms and spreading a disfiguring acne among a group of Soviet spies known to be working within the communist diplomatic corps. The plan was to disfigure the diplomats so badly that their poise at the conference table would be destroyed and they would be sitting ducks for an American proposal to dismember the Warsaw Alliance.

The cunning little mutant that was conjured up in the Salt Lake City research center was accidentally unleashed on the world when a lab assistant sneezed into a petri dish.

The new organism went hunting for a suitable host population. It found it in the hot, sweaty, venereal miasmas of puke rock nightclubs all around the Great Lakes basin. FSU students haunted puke rock clubs.

One of Spent's visitors was a dark, diminutive, Dravidian-looking young man of nineteen. He was a student in Spent's remedial logic class. Dressed in soiled seersucker shorts, he leaned one shoulder against the door jamb, a kind of amused curiosity permanently set on his face. The other was a huge, grinning Nordic churl staring through dirty blond bangs. He wore a red nylon windbreaker with the sleeves torn off, exposing lumpy, threatening biceps. A small American flag was tattooed on his lower arm, the scroll beneath it reading, "Don't Shit on Me."

"I'm here to thank you, doc," the blond said to Spent.

"Thanks?" Spent was bewildered, but relieved. He had expected to be mugged.

"For the recipe."

"I'm not a doctor. I'm ABD—all but the dissertation. Recipe?"

"I'm Richie Fromel," said the blond, grinning. This here's Eddie Mocha."

Spent was bowled over. "Well, this is a . . . a . . ." he stammered.

"Pleasure, right? I'm Vi's baby brother. Majorin' in cookin'. Takin' an M.A. in fast-food hamburger recipes. And some of the way-out stuff, like that horsenpeffer recipe you got hold of. Thought she told you."

"She did. Yes, come to think of it, she did. She cares deeply about you."

"I care for her too, doc, or prof, or whatever. She saved my ass more'n once."

"She's a fine woman. We will be going to the theater tonight, then to dinner."

"Great," said Richie.

Mocha broke in. "Rich's here to let you know we evened it up for you."

"Evened it up?" Spent was having trouble, too much coming at him too fast.

"That asshole dean. Puffit. Worked the little prick over. Caught him out there, right out there in the Plaza of Inspirations. That was one inspiration that come to me in a flash, soon's I saw the little shit." Richie pointed out the window. "First real inspiration ever come to me on that plaza."

Spent was dumbfounded.

"That recipe saved my ass, doc. I passed that Masters cookin' course with honors. Teacher said it was the best recipe any student come in with in years. So I'll be gettin' my graduate degree on time, like I planned. This whole thing at FSU took me almost a year. I'll be leavin' soon. Too fuckin' hot around here. Goin' north. I'd take Vi along but she won't go. Somethin' to do with that fat bastard she works for at The Heist. Name's Stoutbottom. He got somethin' over her."

Spent stumbled to his chair and sat down slowly. "Then it wasn't the memo..."

"Like they say, direct action," said Eddie, walking on his lines.

"Community involvement, like they say," Richie added. "No pissin' around. And we threw up a few pickets around that administration building too. Eddie here made up some of the best signs. One said, 'PUFFIT FUCKS VIRGIN MONKEYS.'"

"And we spray-canned the shit out of the lower floor of that building," said Mocha proudly.

"Wasted your time on that," Richie said. "Next day the art prof's out there sittin' on the grass with his class. Seminar on graffiti."

"How did you know I was in jail?" Spent asked.

"Word gets around fast, doc," Richie said.

Spent's spirits began to sink. "Then it was not the memorandum that..."

"Memo? Shit, no," said Mocha. "We didn't send him nothin'. We just put up them pickets. Then we caught him and beat the piss out of him. We told him we wanted him to understand the due process."

"All that tight argumentation..." Spent's mind was wandering.

"Nobody was tight, doc. We just let Puffit know you got friends," said Mocha.

"Were you gentlemen involved...I mean, did you gentlemen figure prominently...that is, did you contribute...to the trashing of the audio-visual center?" Spent asked, hoping to get a lead.

"Shit, no," said Mocha. "That was some guys from off the campus. They said they thought this campus was too snobbish. Students braggin' about how many movies they got to see here to get their degrees. Senseless fuckin' violence, like they say."

"Well, we gotta move along," said Richie. "Anything else we can do for you, doc, just let us know. Anything you want, just sing out."

"I could use tenure..." Spent's mind was drifting. A wonderful city of dreaming spires seemed to hang in the air before him. A wide yellow-brick road seemed to open before it.

"Tenure?" asked Richie. "What in hell is that?"

"A special kind of license," said Spent dreamily.

Richie shook his head. "You okay?"

"Okay," said Spent, his thoughts back under control.

"We gotta haul ass," said Mocha.

Richie and Spent shook hands. "I like the idea of a doc in the family," said Fromel, "even if you ain't a doc."

Richie and Eddie broke into song as they moved down

the hall toward the elevators. It was the melody from a puke rock classic, now almost two weeks old. "We gonna be free. You and me, babe. You fuckin'-A, babe. This is the American way, babe."

Spent had never liked puke. In fact he detested it. But this tune seemed different. He thought he heard a tiny fragment of César Franck's D minor in it. It had a stately, measured quality, andante in tempo. If you left out the throwing up, he thought, puke might not be such a plague after all...

He settled into his office chair. Realization that he had not earned his freedom but was given it by two young thugs settled across his world of dreams and ambitions like a layer of mildew. He could feel the gloom settle over him. This blow had come, after all, hard on the heels of the collapse of his rabbit-ranching scheme. He thought momentarily, sympathetically, of the disappointment President Kempt must have felt when the Antarctic heat-pump plan fell through and mobs chased him back to his helicopter. That was the kind of disappointment he knew he had to learn to live with. In fact, the whole world seemed to be succumbing to disappointment. It was not just wars and rumors of wars, Christs and anti-Christs locked in a final titanic struggle. It was a series of short but continuous disappointments, small by themselves, but frightening in implication, like beer going stale just before it turns skunky.

The only bright spot in Spent's cubbyhole office was his porcelain coffee cup. He picked it up, eyed it lovingly, then set about heating some water in his instant coffeemaker.

How he loved that coffee cup. It was the only thing he had of his father's. When his mother died it was the only thing that escaped the auction block. The small bluebird that soared across its alabaster sky seemed like an angel from a medieval altarpiece. As a boy, he had watched that same serene bird fly to and from its nest in the wooden fence post behind the house. He would sit in the deep grass near the house and watch it by the hour, coming and going. As it returned to nest it would cut an azure parabola low across the meadow green. The bird would hover magically, its wings fluttering once or twice, then disappear into the nest.

Later, when Spent was in graduate work and the Latin term *raptus* was described to his class by Professor Deborah Fanview, the word stuck in his mind like a tiny pinwheel of light. *Raptus,* rapture, was the direct vision of God and things divine, according to Bacon. The highest of seven grades of interior experience. Spent came to associate it with medieval paintings of the Virgin in blue and scarlet and gold—and with the memory of the bluebird.

Back in June of 1995, the day the newspapers announced that the Audubon Society had officially confirmed the extinction of the bluebird, Spent had broken down and cried publicly for the first time in his life. It was the monotonous beat of the wheels of the old train that got to him. They seemed to mock him as he wept, *"Raptus . . . Raptus . . . Raptus,"* then "I told you so . . . I told you so . . . I told you so."

Spent's weeping had interrupted a birthday party for Jerry, the retiring railroad conductor. Someone had brought a birthday cake on board, with Fourth of July sparklers alight on top of it. When the passengers began to sing, the conductor, four ten-year service stars on his sleeves and a threadbare blue serge vest covering a heart grown threadbare by years of enforced amiability, had broken down and wept. And Jerry thought Spent was weeping for him because everyone knew that retirement no longer meant a deck chair and a mint julep, but scrounging and wheedling and trying to make it to the grave on a full stomach. It had been a trying moment for both of them, embracing, weeping, chucking each other under the chin, bucking each other up.

All during the performance of *Midnight and the Gastropod,* Violet kept leaning over to whisper bar-napkin jokes into Spent's ear.

"What's perpetual motion, Cass?"

"Shhhhh."

"Give up?"

"I give up."

"It's not a cow drinking milk, silly."

"Shhhhh."

"It's you and me in each other's arms."

And all during the long scene in which the brother and sister stand nude watching the fish tank snails, she rubbed her ankle up and down the side of Spent's bare leg.

Both Spent and Violet were stripped down to underwear, as were most people in the theater. Here and there a couple wore short-sleeved blouses and summer-weight slacks, holdouts in the with-it crowd. Everyone else had taken most of his or her clothes off.

The men were mostly pot-bellied with saggy pectorals, moles and patches of graying body hair. Some were skinny and knock-kneed. Many were bald and a few sported beards, though the heat wave had largely ended the full beard and shoulder-length hairdo on all but the obstinate young. Some wore bikini shorts with large, swaggering Corinthian-leather codpieces sewn to the fronts. The latest thing, Spent had read, in from the theaters and cafes of Europe.

The women appeared fat and bluish for the most part. Some were tormented by heat rash and carried small cans of talcum powder, an increasingly expensive amenity. They would douse themselves, scratch, smile wanly, a distant hint of despair in their eyes, then douse themselves again.

In the expensive box seats, as further evidence of affluence, a small white cloud of talc seemed to hover over the seats.

Some women wore bras, assorted G-string arrangements and the crotchless short-shorts that were so big in Nome. The breasts of others sagged alarmingly, implying ballast of some sort. Violet whispered to Spent that they were the ones who went for the postindustrial plastic that promptly degenerated into heavy pebbles of resin—the reason it had finally been withdrawn from the market. Other women, wraithlike anorexics with dark, heavily charcoaled eyes, wore enormous artificial breasts beneath thin gauzy brassieres. They were evidence of a new do-it-yourself fad started by an enterprising cosmetic firm. The corporation marketed balsa-wood and airplane-glue kits that allowed women to design the size and shape of breast they desired. It resulted, of course, in a great range of cubes, pyramids and geodesics.

The result of all the undressing was not a kind comment on a creature that was supposed to be created in the image of God. Or, at any rate, thought Spent, God seemed to be a singularly saggy, bulging and blotchy prototype. The undressing was all done, of course, in the name of the new honesty of the nineties, in the name of acceptance, the frank and honest acceptance of the human body, moles, folds, warts and all. It was not done to celebrate the Creator's triumph during Genesis. For Spent, the trouble was that he had not suspected that moles, folds and warts were so common, and he had trouble holding in mind Leonardo's drawing of spread-eagled man, muscular, balanced, beautifully aligned within a circle of perfection. And for Spent the theater suddenly took on a ridiculous quality. He felt embarrassed at being there, despite the jokes and banter before the lights went down and the occasional pinch and squeal he saw and heard after the curtain had gone up.

Violet's body was beautiful, still snug and tight within

its skin. Her legs and thighs were firm and vigorous-looking and her breasts, the nipples pressing through the thin gauze bra she wore, were large but neither pretentious nor presuming. The general effect on Spent was one of excitement. He knew enough about psychoanalysis, including its various recent forms, not to dwell on why her fanny, in particular, interested him. For one thing he could remember his father, drunk, once calling his mother an "old leather ass" in front of him. Then she beat the man senseless with a kitchen stool.

Each time Violet turned toward Spent and brushed him with her shoulder he would swallow, his saliva would thicken and the word *tumescence* would rumble into his consciousness. Near the middle of the first act, Spent was getting desperate.

Midnight and the Gastropod never really interested Violet, nor did sitting in a sea of fussing, talcum-dousing, half-naked theater lovers. But aroused men did interest her. Twice, when Spent lost complete track of what was going on on the stage and looked at her—the sun, the moon and the stars all crowding into his lovestruck eyes—she glanced at his crotch and whispered, "I bet we don't make it through the second act." He gritted his teeth and fastened with renewed determination onto Karmel's towering theatrical metaphor of copulating snails. But Violet played on Spent's desperation with the glee of a child poking an anthill with a stick. "Bet we don't," she repeated every few minutes.

And they didn't. Spent and Violet left the theater at the end of the first act, grabbed a cab and headed for her apartment. In the cab everything that was good seemed to overwhelm Spent's mind and emotions: the bluebird's flight; great paintings he had seen, especially the nudes; the heroic periods in great men's lives, like Mahler cooped up all alone in the little composing hut outside Vienna, repeating the lines of Li Po's poetry as he composed his

Songs of the Wayfarer; and the story of how Li Po had drowned reaching for the reflection of the moon in the water; the night sky, even if a space platform fled across it every few hours, a great tangle of tawdry junk upon a velvet heaven; and memories of good old Harry, sentimental and wet-eyed every time someone mentioned children, kittens, God or bock beer.

It was obvious to Spent that Violet Fromel was a well-paid waitress. The apartment building was located only a couple of blocks back from the lake near the old Windermere Hotel. Its small front lawn and barberry bushes were immaculately groomed. And the lobby was not just any lobby. The carpet was deeply sculptured with large rose patterns. The lounge chairs were upholstered in a bold zebra-print fabric. A huge marble urn near the elevator held a convincing artificial fanleaf palm. Two large mirrors of deep blue glowed from floor to ceiling on each of the side walls. The inner security doors were of heavy blue glass with illustrations of Romans in an advanced state of cultural decline—drinking, dancing nude, quaffing flagons of wine, strumming lyres, crawling over one another.

The apartment itself was richly appointed in the same style as the lobby. The bedroom, to which Violet dragged Spent without ado, was sumptuous. There was a canopy over the bed, an enormous vanity near it, wallpaper with illustrations of Ronald Colman's motion picture love scenes. With a flip of a switch the hi-fi system went on. Of all things, Sinatra. His music was pretty well forgotten in the nineties, but here and there, in odd little places, some bars, some homes—nursing homes in particular—it could still be heard.

"Love ol' Frankie," said Violet kicking off her shoes and throwing herself on the bed. "You?"

"Sure. I don't remember much of his stuff."

"Well, this will just keep going, so don't worry." She pulled Spent over on top of her.

It was your usual love scene, a mixture of tenderness, bravado, intensity, rolling, pitching, yawing, sighing, self-concern, duty, contentment, smugness, more tenderness, dozing, play, inquiries, jokes about salesmen and comments on the weather.

Violet was sitting on the edge of the bed then, explaining to Spent why the apartment was not just any apartment.

"Cass," she said, a small chuckle bubbling up, "a person has got to be a realist. If a woman is going to have men she might as well get something practical out of it. The fun isn't enough. But you're lots of fun. You need some lessons, but you're okay. Living is mostly a mirage, ya know. It's all up here." She pointed at her head. "Not this. This ain't no mirage." She pinched Spent in the groin. Then, out of nowhere it seemed, there was the sound of the knocker on the apartment door. "Oh, my God," Violet whispered, "that ain't no mirage either."

There was the sound of the slow, deliberate insertion of a key. The lock snapped, sharp, metallic-sounding, and there were footsteps. Spent rose, sat transfixed next to Violet on the side of the bed.

It was Ted Stoutbottom, the Toad, standing in the doorway of the bedroom, heavy-eyed and malevolent, his arms folded.

"Well, Spent," Stoutbottom said, "you look better with your clothes on." Without a glance in her direction he leveled a sharp, backhanded slap at Violet's cheek. And, casually, with the taut power of a snarling jungle cat, he punched Spent in the eye. Spent somersaulted backward over the bed onto the floor. He shook his head as the brilliant orange blur in his brain cleared.

"Mr. Stoutbottom," Spent stammered. "Sir... Sire."

He hoped to make a case for love and laughter on a pleasant evening in July in Chicago.

Violet, of course, was doing her best to be helpful. She sat in a chair on the far side of the bed, shivering and weeping.

Stoutbottom walked around the bed, positioned himself above Spent like the Colossus of Rhodes and casually drove his fist into Spent's face again, this time on the nose.

"Toad, I mean Ted, listen!" Spent pleaded. The difference in mode of address proved important. Spent received a nasty kick in the ribs that sent him scuttling across the floor to the far end of the room where he came up in a half-seated position against the hi-fi console. Sinatra was singing "You Turned My World Around." But it was small consolation.

Stoutbottom smiled. "Just tryin' to freshen your memory, prof."

The mention of memory seemed to Spent to be an opening, some small invitation to negotiation. He addressed the Toad on memory, hurriedly, citing Emerson's essay on circles, trying to draw away a beast's savagery with commentary on a sparkling gem from the world of great literature. He told Stoutbottom that memory was like a circle, that it was a vast container of the spirit that stored a record of both good and evil deeds, and that if untempered by the good, compassion primarily, the entire thing would become a festering compost heap of wrongs.

Stoutbottom was not impressed. "The only Emerson I know is the prissy sonofabitch tending bar at your dinky little faculty club." He picked up Spent's clothes and threw them at him.

Violet whimpered, "Ted, I wasn't doing anything wrong. I need time off too, you know."

"You love me. You work for me!" said Stoutbottom.

"You ask this jerk to put up fifty dollars for this 'time off?' Hell, no, you didn't. I know, 'cause I got word about you fixin' up this date. You didn't say nothin' to me Vi, nothin'. That any way to treat the man you love?" He paused.

"I think Cass is a fine man, Ted," said Violet. "Maybe he ain't the businessman you are, but he's nice. Someday, somehow, I'm going to make it up to him for what you did. Beating him up like this."

"Didn't hurt the skinny fart. Just cleared his sinuses. You think he's so damned nice, ask him to pay for this spread you got here. Ask him!"

Spent was silent. Sinatra was still turning the world around.

Stoutbottom moved to the doorway. "From now on, Spent, you want to do free push-ups you go down to the Y."

"That's a damn cheap shot at the youth of America," Spent managed to say.

"Now get your skinny ass out of here," Stoutbottom said as he ushered Spent half-dressed to the hall, shoved him out of the apartment and slammed the door behind him.

The elevator across the hall was in motion, about to release a load of passengers. Spent made a dash for the stairwell, closed the fire door behind him and leaned on it while he put on his pants and shirt. He had left his shoes in Violet's apartment.

On the train, Spent dabbed his eye with a dampened handkerchief. It had almost closed. Otherwise, apart from sore ribs, he felt reasonably good. He had never been beaten up before and he had imagined it would be worse.

At Tremont he got off the train, walked painfully, his toes curled like a chimp's, across the gravel of the roadbed to the blacktop road that led into the park. He followed the road to the high dunes and headed for a blowout he had often visited on Sundays. The warm, wind-chastened saucer of sand welcomed him like an old friend. He collapsed onto the sand and slept.

When Spent woke the east was turning bright blue and pink and the sun, still below the horizon, cast a small halo of light yellow above the dunes. The throb behind his eye seemed to invite the horrors of the night before back into his mind.

There were two things Spent remembered. One was Violet's beauty and helplessness as she sat naked and shivering in the bedroom chair at the vanity. The other was that he had made no effort to fight back when the Toad assaulted him. Stoutbottom was big, true, but he was a bucket of lard. A hard punch in the gut would probably have floored him. But all Spent had done was try to lecture Stoutbottom on Emerson's theory of circles, which was as useless as trying to teach Puffit the meaning of the wheel and the mirror.

The implications of his cowardice were deeply troubling to Spent. The heart of the matter seemed to have something to do with glimpses into his father's character he had gotten as a boy during those long sessions in the bar. For if some other habitué of Kodesh's took exception to what Harry said about somebody's relatives or wife, Harry would instantly back down, deflecting the threat with specious amiability. If someone suggested that he would punch Harry in the eye if he opened his mouth again, or if Kodesh implied he just might throw Harry out the back door if he didn't stop making a nuisance of himself, Harry would turn on the charm and hide behind that curious grandiosity. And there was that sweet sadness of permanent indecision hanging over everything his father did...

Spent's realization that he, too, toyed with life, that the remark he had given the unicorn just a week before so that the unicorn could give it back to him and make them both feel good—the grand assertion that "The life of the adventurer is nothing but the practice of the art of the impossible"—was lifted, in fact, from a leucocholic nineteenth-century theologian who also toyed with life, hit Spent like Stoutbottom's fist. The nineteenth-century man of faith was so afraid of life he would not marry the woman he loved. He chose instead to trivialize his existence by writing books that were too confused to be clearly pointless. And that realization—that he, too, used his inspirations as an excuse to avoid his own life—sank to the center of his soul like a hot volcanic stone.

But there did seem to be two things at that moment that Spent considered utterly impossible, impossible enough to call out the adventurer in him. One was to save Violet from the Toad. The other was to save America from the likes of Puffit and Kempt.

CHAPTER 11

"There's only one way to win her back, one way to win her heart."

"What is it, Del? For God's sake, tell me."

"Build her a nest."

"A nest?"

"A house."

"A house?"

"A home."

Delbert Dooley and Casper Spent were on the six o'clock train as it scraped and grunted toward Tremont. Spent hadn't seen Dooley for weeks.

"I don't understand."

"Take it from me, Cass. I've thought about it. Women are nesting creatures, all of them. Home and hearth is their reason for being."

Spent didn't take Dooley seriously. "Women are important, all right. Schopenhauer said, 'Without women, the beginning of our life would be helpless; the middle, devoid of pleasure; and the end, of copulation.' I mean... 'consolation.'"

Dooley smiled tolerantly. He would give Spent a chance to settle down.

"The krauts were right, Del. You know what they've always said. The big three for women are kindergarten, *kirche*. . . and automated kitchen."

"Well, if I could get Kay back I'd settle for any part of the triangle," said Dooley, half seriously.

"Kay turned her back on her nesting urge, right, Del? Refused to face it. And position is everything in nesting," said Spent, stretching the conversation to where it threatened to break in half.

"Did you know she's in the hospital? All that partying, all that drinking. The drugs. She went to every damn space-bust Pester could find."

The "space-bust" was a spin-off from puke rock. Young people dressed up in costumes that imitated 1980 space fantasy movies, drank and drugged themselves into a stupified state and talked about coitus. Some tortured themselves and each other with all varieties of weird high-tech devices especially designed for "party-time America," small, ornately decorated forceps, pocket-sized, battery-driven devices that heated up like hair curlers, tiny gouges and hooks. Some party-goers were maimed from repeated space-busts. Most simply got sick or went into a kind of dull-eyed stupor much admired on the West Coast.

Spent realized Dooley was serious. "Kay will be all right," he said, touching his friend's arm reassuringly. He did not believe it, of course.

"She picked up some damn new bug. Hospital says they can't knock it out. New resistant strain that shows up in pork. They say her immune system is shot."

"That goes for the whole damn society, Del. We're not immune anymore to the rubbish coming out of our writers and painters, or the media. Laboratories too, for that matter."

"I'm hoping there will be a breakthrough. In time for Kay."

"Another breakthrough could finish us all off."

"Well, perhaps. But I've been doing a lot of thinking."

"That's a start."

"Seriously, Cass, for God's sake. And reading too. The country is in terrible shape, so is most of the world. We're breeding like microbes. We've practically destroyed the planet."

"One more reason why we don't need atomic weapons."

"Will you be serious, for Christ's sake?"

"For His sake only."

"Well, just look at it. Nothing you don't know, but just look at it. We've killed damn near every wild animal off. It's like you say. In places like Nepal they're hunting down the last stick of wood for fuel to cook. In this country we paved over most of our good land, or crapped it up with poison."

Dooley paused, unbuttoned his shirt almost to the waist and fanned himself clumsily with a magazine, a copy of *Futureweek*. A puke rock star was featured in the cover story. He had become famous by delicately blending the sound of his howls with the recorded sounds of his bowel movements. He was, the magazine noted, an overwhelming success.

"Like the wit says, Del, 'An optimist is the man who hasn't heard the latest news.' The trouble is in our high-tech hearing aid."

"Well, it won't blow over. It hasn't and it won't."

Neither man spoke for a long time as the train ground along.

"There's a sense of evil hanging over the whole thing," said Dooley, his fists clenching. "That's the worst part. I hear those Washington people lie in their teeth and I sometimes think the devil has taken possession of them."

Spent was surprised at the intensity of his friend's feelings. He had felt many of the same fears, and much of the bitterness. But he hadn't realized Dooley was turning radical. And his own feelings were still cocooned in the gauzy sentiments of the scholar's outlook on life, his love of decline-and-fall theories, Gibbon, Spengler, Brooks Adams... Adams's *The Law of Civilization and Decay*. Even the title was beautiful, like a Piranesi etching of a decaying Roman temple, melancholy, overgrown with vegetation, a goatherd and his flock loafing in the shadows of ancient majesty. He loved the feeling of the inexorability of it all. For inexorability was the one thing no romantic could live without. It produced the lassitude of spirit he loved. It excused everything, forgave everything, made duty complicated and elusive. It allowed one to put bombastic capitals on words like Will and Fate, and Great, so that their simple meaning could be evaded. In terrible times it made things easy. "There is a certain—" He was about to say something about old Harry. Something sentimental.

"—Evil is not certain," Dooley interrupted. "If it was, we couldn't choose it. Evil requires *choice*. It lives on choice; it feeds on choice."

Spent felt embarrassed. With Dooley *he* had always done the real talking. Now Dooley had taken hold of his own ideas, firmly, even fiercely. "You think the devil is real? I mean... evil?" asked Spent, his voice low, almost apologetic.

"I really don't know. But I do know the world is being destroyed by something in man. It's like a rot. Like a rotting corpse polluting a river. The smell of death hangs over everything, including that ridiculous FSU. 'Evil' is all I can call it. When people say there is no such thing as evil, because everything has a cause, I just think of Nazis hanging Jews with piano wire. It clears my head!"

Spent looked at Dooley as if he had just been introduced to him.

"Whatever it is, it's loose in the world, and we all know it. It's as if the devil were trying to prove he still has power, using a ruined world as his credentials. That's why you must build that home for Violet. It'll scratch a line off the goddamned devil's resume."

Dooley sounded positively profound to Spent. So Spent went rummaging hurriedly through his memory to try to top him. There was a line from George Eliot hovering somewhere, about the growing good of the world being the result of small unhistoric acts. He could not fully retrieve it. But he did realize at that moment that the same thing could be said for the growth of evil.

Spent knew Dooley was thinking of Kay, wanted to talk more about her. "She'll be all right. Your wife, I mean."

Dooley was staring out the window now, watching a row of army trucks inching through Gary. There had been riots or something. "I stopped at the hospital this morning to see Kay. Surprised her. She was reading an old copy of *Lovely Homes,* a special issue on kitchens from the eighties. She was crying. She loved that stuff. Pictures of fuzzy animals... rose arbors, little girls in ruffled frocks carrying watering cans. English perennial gardens, cottages... mossy shingles, big iron hinges on the doors."

Spent was moved by Dooley's descriptions of what he had loved so much in Kay. He liked women who liked the same sort of thing. Perhaps, thought Spent, it was the key to their friendship. "Old geezers in buttoned cardigans, carrying walking sticks," Spent added.

"Words like *fetch* and *bucksaw.*"

"I know what you mean. Words like *cowslip* and *husbandry*. Balloon rides over Iowa on a warm day in June, back in the seventies."

"I may join the New Ludd movement, Casper," said Dooley abruptly, opening the vent in the balloon, letting it return to earth with a thump.

"I should build a house for Violet—is that what you're saying?" asked Spent, almost oblivious to Dooley's statement, but back on the ground.

"Women want more than a screw, Cass. They want their love *in* a nest."

"Can't face her. The way I handled that whole thing with Stoutbottom..."

"She still cares about you, Cass. She wouldn't have acted the way she did if she didn't care." It was Dooley's turn to lie a little.

"Houses cost a fortune, Del. And I am out of work, you know."

"You've got a few thousand stashed away. You told me."

"My money wouldn't put a patch on a mortgage."

"I'm into woodwork now, Cass, as a hobby—for this damned itch. You could build a house a lot easier than you think. I'd throw in a few Saturdays myself. Swag would too."

Spent realized Dooley was serious. "You mean the old bowerbird caper?" he asked, amused, buoyed up.

"Never heard of bowerbirds."

"They were real birds, wings, feathers, beaks, that sort of thing. They're gone now. They used to live in New Guinea. Magnificent creatures. Rather like birds of paradise. Instead of evolving that wonderful plumage they built bowers of twigs, sticks, colored stones, flowers. The male attracted the female that way." He paused, mopped his brow with his handkerchief. "You may have something about the house thing."

"All people ever want is a home. That's why they used

to want to come to this country. A lot still do. America used to be one big home, with the welcome mat out."

"Now it's one big, leaking, sanitary landfill."

"With lumber prices what they are," said Dooley, "you should find an old building, perhaps a farm building. Take it apart, move it to the dunes and put it back together."

"How the hell would I find an old farm building?" There's damn little that hasn't been scrounged off the countryside by people trying to patch up their homes."

"Use your head. You'll find what you want."

Spent and Dooley didn't speak for the next half hour. Dooley had dozed off, sitting upright. Spent brought him around with an elbow to the ribs. "I think I've got it, Del. I think I do. Submarine warfare!"

"Submarine warfare?"

"Sure, the classic needle-in-a-haystack strategy. Finding a target out in the middle of nowhere. I'll have to review the idea of Erich Raeder and Karl Dönitz. Perhaps Günther Prien as well." Spent puckered his mouth around the umlauts.

"Jawohl," Dooley answered, shaking his head, still slumped in his seat.

"I really do think I've got it." Spent was excited

"I know you've got it," said Dooley. "Bad." He grinned and dozed off again.

That night Spent stayed up pouring over highway maps of northern Indiana and Illinois. He prepared a large transparency to go over each map, with a ten-mile-square grid over each. By dawn he was finished. He added decorative touches to the borders of the maps, a balloon-cheeked face blowing down from the north, two sea serpents and sprays of deadly nightshade in bloom at the corners.

Then he napped for two hours, rose and prepared sandwiches of cheese and cucumber laminated with smears of mustard. He began driving at six-thirty that morning, working southward, sweeping one square on the grid at a time.

Nothing turned up for the first two days out, Wednesday and Thursday. On Friday, Spent came across an old frame building on the grounds of an abandoned Spanish-American War veteran's center. A small commune of squatters, Floridians, former real estate developers, were living in it. They were red-eyed, tattered, half drunk and bellicose. Growls, curses and threats followed Spent's questions about ownership, asking prices and plat numbers. To the leader of the group Spent was "obviously a socialist sonofabitch."

On Saturday, Spent found a large, abandoned chicken coop. The cages were still intact. So was the space-age Skinnerian electrical system used to shock hens into laying their eggs prematurely so that the shell remained soft and could be ground into cake mix without the cost of cracking the eggs. But the coop reeked with a pungent ammonia smell welling up from large piles of chicken dung in the corners of the building. It brought tears to Spent's eyes.

The chicken coop, too, had become part of America's housing stock. On the north side of the coop a family of poverty-stricken Arizonans had rigged a lean-to of old boards and scraps of canvas. They were friendly. They invited Spent to join them for iceless Kool-Aid and unbuttered brown bread. They were, they said, former operators of a curio shop in Scottsdale. Curios were about all they knew, they said. One of them was already busy making small models of the national capitol from stacks of abandoned egg cartons. Their intention was to protect the chicken coop from lumber scavengers until the odor had subsided and they could fix it up as a home and roadside curio stand.

On Sunday afternoon, Spent went to his favorite spot in the dunes to rest. He lay in the shade of a small shagbark oak and stared at the sky for hours, pondering the life of the adventurer. He napped for several hours. When he awakened, he raised himself on one elbow and watched a solitary ship disappear to the north over the horizon of Lake Michigan. It moved silently, ignoring the world. Late in the afternoon the sun began to settle toward the west, a ball of brilliant yellow encased in concentric rings of rose and gold. With the sandstorms in the prairie states, sunsets around Chicago had become spectacular.

On Monday he rose early and continued the search. Nothing turned up that morning. All afternoon, back and forth, in and out of main roads, side roads, abandoned roads, he drove. Then, without warning, as he rounded a curve in grid 646–BN (meaning the six-hundred-forty-sixth grid examined, B subgrid, north) it announced itself. It stood in a five-acre, treeless field, in a sea of cockleburrs and goldenrod, a great long half-log building. Scavengers had somehow missed it. It was mellowed by time; most of the roof joists had caved in. It was an abandoned horse barn. It had eleven great stalls, massive timber studding and great steel tie rods from eave to eave. Spent knew instantly that it would be a simple matter to remove the stalls when he rebuilt the barn and reassembled them in staggered combinations, creating natural and free parcels of living space, in the prairie architecture tradition of Wright.

And near the horse barn, once a strong and serviceable companion to a cow barn, long since torn down, stood an old silo of stone, large and squat, every inch a testament to some man's life as an adventurer. It would be taken down stone by stone and put together again as a study, something set apart from the house, as a place to think and write, alone and yet connected by a drawbridge, an umbilicus to the world that he and Violet would share. A world of soft moments, warm kitchens, barley soup, home-baked bread and Violet's Sinatra collection. A circular stair would lead to the topmost chamber of the silo. There Spent would sit in solitude and create, like Montaigne and Joyce in their towers, while the noise of brazen ambition clanged in the world outside.

It was four hours before Spent was able to locate the owner of the property, a cataract-eyed old man residing in Valparaiso, living on supply-side sacrifice, mostly Purina Cat Chow, in a closed gasoline station. They clinched the deal over a handshake and a cup of weak tea. Spent bought the building for $1,900.

That night Spent's journal became the diary of the building of a bower.

June 25

A welcome chance comment at Kunst's bar tonight. Rumors that federal parkland will be sold for almost nothing. Kunst's sister Gertrude offered to sell a half acre near here, just outside the park, for a song. Settled the deal on the spot. The lot is swampy and overgrown with bullthistles. Will call our new home "Thistledown."

July 26

Swag enthusiastic about Thistledown. Says it will do for me what his home did for him and Dorothy.

Eddie Nettles will work for me too, for five dollars a day. What a guy! Loves the impossible. Loves to work with crews. Used to hang around Kunst's hoping for a crisis, a blizzard or a flood, or a chance to direct traffic at the county fair.

Won't wear his false teeth.
Horse barn doesn't smell at all.

July 27

Dog-tired. Swag and Eddie borrowed Kiefhaufer's truck. Their help invaluable. Most of the material moved.

July 28

Swag expresses concern about my spending all my savings on materials. Love the way he put it. "You're talkin' big money, Cass, not just nickels and dimes. You may have to float a loan to finish. When you're floatin' a loan that size you're treadin' thin water."

July 29

Huge pile of timber, boards, tie rods, odds and ends in the lot, along with new materials.

July 30

Used the day to prepare more plans. Into Chicago to scour architecture literature. Characteristics of barn somewhat restrictive. Palladio of little use. Jefferson's approach to Monticello inappropriate. He had a hill; I have a hollow.

August 3

My apologies, Journal. Tied up. FSU investigation of A-V break-in and beating of Puffit. Worry at the possibility that Richie may meet specifications of the transom unit measure. But he is innocent!

Something going with Kastowitz and Puffit. Richie says they're into narcotics traffic, and selling paraquat weed killer to police. Working both sides of the street.

Richie says Violet punched around again by Stoutbottom. Wants to see me. I am happy beyond belief.

Thistledown ahead of schedule.

August 4

Swag is a man! "They'll have a big Caterpillar on your lot tomorrow," he announced at dinner tonight. "They'll go down four foot for the crawl space and footings. Nettles knows how to handle Cats. Cost you nothin' but the price of the diesel fuel."

Dorothy ecstatic. Swag told her I had marriage plans.

August 5

Dooley spent the entire day with me and Swag, setting foundations. Loves the name "Thistledown." Wishes his house had a name. Calls it "the empty place."

His itch is better. Fresh air and work seem to help.

Went to beach with Swag, Dorothy, Del and the kids. Swag looks like a potbellied Greek god. Kids swarmed all over Del. Love him. He's an uncle to them.

Scum on water, drifting in from Chicago area, cut the swimming short. Not as many dead fish as last year. Dead fish always hopeful sign. The lake is not entirely sterile.

August 6

Wrote poem "To the Wood Duck." Called Violet from the office. "Must see you, darling."

Will see her tomorrow at Tudor's at three.

August 7

This will be a long entry, Journal.

Arrived at Tudor's at 2:30, on the safe side. Place almost empty. At four, she was still not there. Had more Turkey. Listened to bartender and supplier. Modern man in search of his soul.

"What about some more vodka?"

"Could use a couple of cases."

"Pride of the Pripet Marsh or Virgin Cassock?"

"One of each."

"Better make it two."

"Okay. Two."

Studied the Tudor's decor for ideas to use in Thistledown. Walls with heavy plaster troweled into giant swirls—reminded me of train conductor's birthday cake. Plastic stained-glass windows lighted from rear. Rob Roy tartan rug. Swords and mugs all over the wall (Swag would love them). Large plaster-of-paris knight, gilt, kneeling in vigil near the cash register. Painting of fat friar on wall. Man of God wrapped in seraphic smile, sipping wine in shadowy wine cellar, eyes on heaven, streak of sunlight bouncing off tonsured pate. Could almost hear sound of matin bells and evening hymns in chapel upstairs.

5:30 P.M.

Still no Violet. My heart has become a laboring pump.

Room began to hum with excitement. After-work boozehounds arriving. A big, good-looking brunette spins through the door. Noisy, well-heeled, clean, hair done up beautifully and sprayed in place. Very self-confident. Probably spayed. Spots friend at bar.

"Joanieeeee! Joanieeeee! Heard you were in town. Great to get your call. I thought you were still up north with that beautiful Greenlander hunk. Saw you, you know, last

March on your catamaran on the Yukon. You didn't see me."

"Don't you think this whole thing with the weather just too ridiculous?"

"Always something. Bill and I are leaving again tomorrow. I can't stand all the pessimism in towns like this. Our place is near Dawson, you know. It's a wonderful upbeat place."

Violet came in at 6:30. She was panting, glowing through her makeup, talking fast. Sounded frightened.

"That big ape said I couldn't see you unless you paid fifty dollars an hour."

"Then leave, for God's sake, Violet. Leave him," I said.

"Well, he won't lower his price."

"He's an insecure, anti-intellectual wretch, Violet. Face it."

"I know, but what can I do? Can't move into the street."

"Marry me."

She thought I was joking. Used a bar-napkin joke. "I got a parrot that swears, a cat that stays out all night and a fireplace that smokes. Who needs a husband?"

"I mean, it, Violet."

"Sure you do, Cass. All men are born free and equal. If they get married later, that's their fault. Right? Got that one on a napkin yesterday."

"I mean it, Violet."

"Oh, my God. Your eye's still swollen. But I wouldn't worry, Cass. The cops are after Ted. He's on probation, you know, for pushing phony dope."

"Will you?"

"Will I?"

"Marry me? I'm building a house. It's called Thistledown."

Her eyes widened and she squealed, "I will, Cass. I will, I will, I will."

We embraced, kissed, kissed again, clung, kissed long and deep.

Bartender whistled. Joanieee stared, raised her eyebrows, began again about the catamaran.

August 10

Too busy to keep up with my notes. Sorry, dear Journal.

After dinner, went over drawings again and innovations. Will eliminate studs altogether. Wall panels of knotty pine to hang directly from rafters to two-by-fours nailed to floor. Swag says it will be noisy. Reminded him that Violet and I would be there alone.

Swag carefully plugged all knotholes in bedroom walls.

August 11

Thistledown a frank and honest building. Swag and Del think it "a bit too much on the shack side." Told them of the work of Robert Venturi. Explained aesthetics of the shed, the shack and the hovel, the whole thing. They took it like gentlemen, which they are, every inch.

Saw the house tonight by moonlight. Horse-barn origins lend monumentality. Late summer flowers glistening among high swamp weeds behind house. Sniffed the lovely saffron head of goldenrod. Brought on an awesome sneezing fit.

August 12

Another innovation in place. Slide-by windows. Ordinary windows placed on their sides. Instead of pushing up, slide them by.

August 13

Bought large used sump pump from Porter Hardware. With drought, sump pumps now very cheap.

Eddie installed it. Had to cut hole through kitchen floor. My plans had not included the pump. Swag and Eddie ribbed me most of the day—until Eddie squashed a finger heaving the damn thing into place. Took him to Valpo Hospital. Swag brought along beer and brandy. We drank B&Bs.

"It'll ease the pain, Ed," said Swag. "Have another jolt. Alcohol kills pain." In a few more miles, "Pains me to see you suffer. I'll join you in a couple of stiff ones. Beer or brandy the best painkiller? A mute question," says Swag, slumped on the floor.

August 14

For some reason fireplace footing has settled on one side. Footing not deep enough? Brickwork out of plumb almost six inches. Drunken-looking fireplace.

Dorothy says tilted fireplace will lend homemade look to Thistledown's great main room. Swag takes economic view of problem. Says guests at parties will go easy on liquor if they think they're already loaded.

Will try ivy planters to obscure tilt. The indoor-outdoor look.

August 17

Trouble today. Swag's hand-fashioned fifteen-foot ladder longer than needed to reach eaves. Nettles decided to use it at a 45-degree angle, to walk it rather than climb it. Fell, carrying bundle of shingles. Came down straddling a rung. Lucky he wasn't castrated. Brought him round with brandy.

Dorothy threw a picnic together in front of Thistledown; sandwiches, cold wieners, potato salad, several packs of beer. Eddie good as new. But his smiles are still weak.

August 18

Trouble again. Gertrude Kunst says Thistledown sits across the lot line of her remaining property. Should have had lot surveyed. Gertrude warns she will sue if I do not buy another lot. Broke. Cannot buy more land.

Only option is to slice off corner of building. Following Frank Lloyd Wright's lead (a truly noble suspicion of corners), we chopped it off. The result? A splendid chamfered form born of necessity.

August 19

More problems. Flip on switch in bedroom, lights go on in kitchen. Switch on in dining room, light goes on in carport. Long sweaty jog to rerun electric cables. Eddie's feelings hurt because I told him I would do it myself this time.

August 20

Dooley says there is talk of using the dunes area as a burial site for the Rockford nuclear reactor now beginning decommission process! Horrors!

August 21

Government offices refuse any information on proposals to use Dunes National Park as site for burial of dead power plant. Dooley says he will fight them to the end, for his own sake as well as others', like Dorothy's and the kids'.

"For you too, Cass," he said. His eyes looked as though they were on fire.

August 22

The fireplace finished, the doors and windows hung. Violet begs to see the house. Tell her she will see it at the housewarming, as engagement gift.

August 25

Violet and I meet in my office. Lovely beyond words. She is afraid to tell the Toad. Looked up toads in the encyclopedia. Skins exude poison called fulfagin, acts the same as LSD. Violet says she would like to give the Toad a trip to end all trips.

Richie and his friend Mocha offer to work on the house for nothing. "Ain't doin' no cookin' right now, anyway," he said when he showed up at the site yesterday. Mocha and Nettles hit it off.

Nettles took a hit of grass from Mocha and spent the afternoon sitting in the brambles swaying, singing something about Mother Nature.

Swag thought Nettles was having some kind of breakdown. "Wrapping just came off old Eddie," he said.

August 26

Dooley shows up with flyers announcing a rally in Chesterton, to stop the plan for using the dunes as a rad-waste dump. Broken spinning wheel plain on the bottom of the handouts! Dooley's eyes on fire again.

August 27

Large tomcat and female, apparently wild, living off mice in swamp near house, living in crawl space. Swag says two or three hussies have joined his harem.

August 28

Moved a sleeping bag into Thistledown. Worry about lumber scavengers. Stories in Chesterton about new wave of poor coming up highways from Terre Haute area.

Tomcat mates with females at night. Rattle of copper cabling would scandalize the dead.

August 29

Richie brings five of his buddies out from Chicago for "coordinated drive" to oust tomcat and harem. Posted a man at each of the four crawl-space vents, then sent Eddie and Mocha into crawl space with a broom. Richie posted "vent guard" at each outlet through foundation to count cats and record color.

Quarrels broke out among guards on final (third) drive. Some cats were "brown," some "brownish." "Trapping an animal that refused to run would be cowardly," said Swag. Richie agreed. "Besides," said Swag, "nothing stinks like a dead cat in a crawl space."

Mission aborted. Cats allowed to stay. Copper tubing secured to prevent rattle.

September 2

Fall term about to begin. Puffit not seen around much. Rumor that he got Jenny Perch pregnant probably exaggerated.

September 3

Spent evening in front of artificial log fire in Thistledown, with Swag and Dorothy, planning housewarming. Guest list now very long. Kunst denizens, Dooley, the Fromels, Del, Richie and friends, Mocha and buddies.

Swag says the big thing would be to invite Puffit and Pester to show them I can rise above petty differences.

Dooley says Puffit's new assignment on the Crisis Commission on Public Information includes preparation of adult-education TV spots to soften public up to burial of dismantled reactors in remaining national parks, including the dunes. FSU to get huge federal audio-visual grant.

September 4

Dooley very angry and upset. Eyes almost frightening. Says someone spreading a story that Thistledown is to be headquarters of New Ludds. Says he is prepared to break off our friendship and move into town to avoid threats to Thistledown.

Nonsense! Will have nothing of it. Besides, I don't believe him.

September 5

Tomcat and female obviously successful pair. Female has kittens. Nesting in pile of rags in corner of carport. Timmy and Kenny beside themselves with joy. Swag and Dorothy say kittens help heal the wound left by loss of Toothie and ranching scheme.

September 7

Cookout at Thistledown. Report of imminent rains has everyone excited. Smoke from the steaks (Dooley must have paid a fortune for the meat) curling up among the rafters of the carport. Swag regales everyone with stories of small-town life, of a dizzy female called "Half Pint," of why he knocked the teeth out of a young fellow who dunned him for balance on old motorcycle.

Timmy and Kenny laugh themselves silly at the great marshmallow chef's hat I wear, along with apron Dorothy made, with a woodchuck appliqued in the center. Nettles full of stories about varmits and polecats. Dorothy misty-eyed.

At seven in evening, three cars roared up and stopped just beyond Thistledown. Dooley says they're workers who fear New Ludds will stop reactor burial plan and put them out of work.

Official housewarming for Thistledown set for September 10, 1997.

CHAPTER 12

Thistledown's house warming was carried to the extreme. Just after midnight on the eleventh day of September a surly band of unemployed Gary workmen, their bellies full of beer and their heads full of tavern-hatched ad hoc social policy, burned it to the ground. Spent was pitched to the brink of catatonic shock; Violet collapsed into a weeping bundle of despair and Delbert Dooley, the victim of an heroic element in his character that neither he nor his friends suspected, was hospitalized with burns over much of his body.

Swag, Spent and Tom Puffit took Dooley, moaning and near shock, to the emergency ward of the hospital in Valparaiso, thirty miles south of Spent's immolated dream. He was administered the latest in burn therapy.

Around one o'clock that morning a Dr. Bliss, one of the increasing number of senior citizens who found it impossible to retire because of what inflation did to their savings, came into the lobby to report to Spent and the others. He was a man of about eighty years but looked younger, at least to the casual glance. Thanks to the growth of underground barter economics, he was able to trade face lifts and transplant surgery with physicians in Chicago. His decrepit, complaining organs were repackaged every few years within the slick astringent skin of the cosmetic surgeon's art.

"Our patient," he began, rocking on the balls of his feet, his hands thrust deep into the pockets of his smock—one of them trembling—"has been made as comfortable as possible."

"How comfortable is that?" Spent asked.

"Very," said the doctor. "He's unconscious."

"Will he make it?" asked Swag.

"Oh, he's still on the make," said the doctor, trying to wink, the tremor now in his head.

Bliss had hoped a little humor might relieve the fears of Dooley's friends, but they were embarrassed and felt sorry for the old man.

The doctor's anxiety about being discarded in a world exhausted by so much progress hung over him like a bad odor. His body was old and wanted to die, but during the 1990s there was nothing much to be gained by dying. Belief in life after death had pretty much disappeared and there was no place for the dead to go. So most old people preferred to stick around and, like Bliss, stoically underwent one transplant, stretch and tie after another. Instead of being able to join a pool of tranquil wisdom from which bewildered youth could draw courage and inspiration, as they had been promised by gerontology, they were little more than a drug on the market, the last thing in the world a culture with a high-tech information at its fingertips needed. So they flung themselves into a sort of geriatric youth cult. They searched tirelessly—if "tirelessly" was the word to describe creaking, anxious desperation—for a fast track that wasn't too tiring. They valiantly sought to convince themselves that something besides oblivion was just around the corner and preened themselves with whatever self-deception advertisers could come up with. In Bliss's case it produced a kind of equivocal hauteur in personal manner. Repeated tucks about the neck forced him to hold his head high, as if he were inordinately proud of lasting as long as he had, while repeated tucks of the crow's feet about his eyes gave him the ingenuous look of a startled nocturnal rodent about to be eaten by an owl.

"Our patient," Bliss continued, wiping a bit of whitish drool from the corner of his mouth, "did not sustain lung injury from hot gases as is often the case in fire bombings. There have been some real breakthroughs, as you know, in the design of chemical incendiaries." He pursed his lips, dabbed away another tag of drool and drew his breath in slowly. "How...ever...our patient did receive burns, largely, I would guess, of the second degree, possibly the first degree, a few if any of the third degree."

Swag shook his head despairingly. "Ol' Del's gettin' the third degree."

Spent, his mind tumbling as one image of horror after another flashed in his head, then splintered, fled and was replaced by another—the picture of Thistledown being devoured by gulps of bloodthirsty flame, Dooley groaning in the back seat of the car on the way to the hospital, the fire engine from Chesterton careening through the night, lights slashing a frenzied sky—stared at the doctor. "You sound like a Mason," he said.

The doctor's trembling subsided for a moment. The question of spiritual credentials seemed to clear his neural pathways momentarily. "I pride myself, sir, on being a man of my time, a scientist. Science does not need temples or rite. The future is our temple and research is our rite."

"But do you believe in God?" Spent asked.

"I believe God is found in the fur on man's tongue," the

physician said sarcastically, trusting his riposte would chasten the display of impertinence.

"I agree," said Spent. "He is everywhere."

"Prove it. Say ahhhh," said the doctor as he turned on his heel and headed down the hall, tacking uncertainly along his fast track.

Swag looked at Spent. "What the hell's goin' on, Cass? Old Del's in there dyin' and you start talkin' philosophy. How about a little respect, for the Christ's sake?" He turned to Puffit, expecting agreement. "Right, dean?"

Puffit shrugged. He had been there before.

What had happened was this: by ten o'clock that night the housewarmer was in full swing. Violet was there as the guest of honor, with Spent having announced to the group that she had accepted his proposal of marriage. She was bright-eyed and bushy-tailed, as they say, dressed in a skimpy red frock lying low across the shoulders. She wore a new pair of Third World pumps and her face was done up spectacularly with heavy brown eye shadow and a streak of yellow down each side of her face, an effect reminiscent of melting lemon sherbet. It was a stunning comment on the impact of puke rock and high fashion on the working girl's pursuit of happiness in the 1990s.

Her brother, Richie, was there, along with his friend Eddie Mocha and three of their buddies. They were all dressed in summer-weight three-piece suits, none of which fitted very well. Richie could not button the vest on his ensemble and Eddie's trousers pinched severely about the crotch. Violet told Spent with a grin that the boys had shoplifted the suits to celebrate the housewarming.

Swag was dressed in his favorite western outfit: a western-styled shirt, neckerchief and trousers tucked into western boots with "Denver World Fair" boldly stitched into the uppers.

Eddie Nettles was there, shaved and wearing his teeth. He was dressed in a bold plaid shirt with great wide suspenders proclaiming his pride as craftsman and adventurer. He and one of Mocha's friends shared a plug of tobacco, now and then excusing themselves to spit into an empty V–8 can Dorothy had thoughtfully placed behind the ivy planter near the fireplace.

Dorothy was there too, of course, deliriously happy as she busied herself with the victuals. A picnic table had been lugged into the main room of Thistledown and was piled high with food, mounds of sliced ham on paper plates, cold beef on platters, assorted casseroles never honored with a name, three or four varieties of potato salad, pickles, olives, Fritos... a veritable Viking feast, lacking only oxhorns brimming with mead, but which shortcoming was met by a pony barrel of beer placed in one corner.

Kunst and his sister, Gertrude, were there. So were Timmy and Kenny, whizzing about with plates of food and showing off the cardboard box full of kittens that had been brought in from the carport.

To almost everyone's surprise Puffit showed up. Richie Fromel and Eddie Mocha took it in stride, since they'd put the muscle on him earlier. "Nothin's too good for Doc," said Richie. "He'll feel better if that asshole Puffit shows up and eats a little crow at the housewarmin'." Pester was there, too. (Ever since the faculty reception Puffit and Pester seemed closer than ever.) And at the housewarming Puffit told Spent that he had decided that bygones should be bygones and that Spent ought to return to FSU and take over the new research and development program in UFO Lifestyles. Spent was bowled over, and at first suspicious. But Dorothy took him aside and reminded him that he needed a job, any job at that point, if he was going to make his dreams at Thistledown come true. Spent and the rest of the party were soon drinking toasts to Puffit, with Dooley toasting the dean as "that distinctive symbol of our age." Puffit loved it.

At ten-thirty gifts were brought in: a gift certificate for a to-be-assembled plastic bookcase from Penney's, from Puffit; a plastic potted plant from the Kunsts; a plastic "instant party bar" that resembled a folding ironing board from Pester; a fluffy "commuter pillow" of the kind popular on the South Shore from Swag and a variety of pots, pans, dried-food catalogues and such from Nettles and Swag's barroom friends.

At eleven o'clock or thereabouts Dooley went to one of the bedrooms and returned with a huge, oddly shaped package. To the oohs and aahs of the gallery he unwrapped it. It was a lamp, about six feet tall. It was made of the giant iron hook Spent had seen Dooley lugging into his house months ago. Dooley had welded the hook to a heavy iron plate, mounted it against a hollow shaft of driftwood, wired it, wrapped it with rope, then topped it with a shade graced with pictures of diesel-driven whaling ships.

Puffit pronounced the lamp a postindustrial *tour de force,* and Dorothy said it was an unafraid statement from Dooley's heart.

"Isn't much of a lamp, Cass," Dooley said, embarrassed by the reception it received. "Got started doing this sort of thing in the crafts class at the high school. Wait until you see the one I'm making now. It's got a cowbell on the pull cord."

"Better to ring a bell than curse the darkness, Del," said Spent as he embraced his neighbor heartily.

It was midnight when a muffled rumble in the crawl space beneath the floor of Thistledown brought the celebration to stunned silence. Swag had been explaining the operation of the gear box on Kiefaufer's truck to Puffit. Eddie Nettles had pulled Gertrude Kunst onto his lap and was tickling her.

The blue-gray smoke that suddenly pushed up through the heat vents was followed by small licks of flame.

Swag was the first to realize what was happening. "Everyone out! Out into the yard!" he bellowed. As an afterthought he shouted, "Bring your drinks!"

There was nervous laughter as the party pushed and shoved through the doorway and into the night. Richie Fromel got off a wisecrack. "When you promised a housewarming, Cass, I never thought you was this serious."

Outside, the group stared at the fire in dumbfounded silence. Violet covered her face with her hands. Dorothy tottered and sank weeping to the ground; Timmy buried his face against his mother's shoulder.

For several minutes there was complete silence, then a loud *whoosh* as another gasoline bomb ignited in the crawl space. Three of the tomcat's harem darted from under the house.

Kenny, wide-eyed with fear, shrieked, "The kitties are in the house! The kitties will burn!"

Dooley, standing next to the boy, laid his hand on Kenny's shoulder. "Easy, son," he said quietly, "I'll get them out." He bolted into the house. There was another, softer explosion. Dooley's silhouette showed through the windows for a moment, then he stumbled, hunched over the box of kittens. When he finally came out of the house his trousers and the back of his shirt were on fire. He put the box down, staggered three or four steps, collapsed and rolled on the ground. Swag, Puffit and Spent pulled off their shirts and stifled the flames that still flickered about his shoes and belt.

Within fifteen minutes Thistledown was ravaged by fire from end to end, and the front yard was as bright as midday. Tom Puffit had taken charge of the crowd. "Back those cars down the road!... Werner, you go call the hospital! . . . Swag, help me get Del into the car . . . Pester, see that the women and children get home! . . . Spent, damn you! Stop stumbling around with your head up your ass. Give us a hand!"

Dooley was loaded into the back seat of Swag's old Chevrolet, where Puffit cradled his head in his lap. Swag drove, Spent sat next to him.

It was an hour later when Dr. Bliss came in to report that Dooley was sedated and unconscious.

Spent, Swagmacher and Puffit did not talk for almost half an hour after Bliss left the lobby. Spent paced the lounge, occasionally going to the revolving door, pushing through it and back into the room. Swag mechanically leafed through a lobby copy of *Man's Great Moments,* a popular monthly of the nineties that concerned itself with the history of such breakthrough achievements as the invention of the ball in roll-on deodorant devices, a hangover prevention inoculation for teenagers and the first use of the integrated electronic circuit and laser which projected a pornographic hologram TV game called "Letscrew" into the American living room.

Puffit sat in silence in one of the large vinyl-covered chairs, his feet thrust forward as he tapped the soles of his loafers together.

"Why did they do it, Swag? Do you think Del was really a New Ludd?" asked Puffit.

"Hell, no, he wasn't no Ludd. There ain't no New Ludd movement. Ain't no NLM at all. Del told me that just the other day. The whole thing got invented by the newspapers. Picked it up from that bunch that picketed the Zion plant. Del couldn't find no leader. They was just a bunch of mad people livin' near that power plant. When he said he wanted to join up, they asked him, 'Join what?' "

"I thought it was an all-out group. What about the insignia they used, that broken spinning wheel thing?"

"Hell, Del had to make that up himself when he started handing out pamphlets," said Swag. "Copied the damn things at FSU. But he found out that people really don't give a damn." He shook his head.

"I suppose he felt he wanted to do something," said Puffit. "A lot of people feel that way. They don't have faith in what put this country where it is today."

Spent, standing next to Swag, fingered an old copy of *Time*. "Where is it?" he asked.

Puffit, fed up with Spent's baiting, but eager to impress Swag, reached for eloquence and missed. "Fact is the country is faced with a multitude of lethargy."

Annoyed, Spent slumped in a chair and covered his eyes with a forearm.

"That's why our GNP has gone down," Puffit went on. "But this is a great country. And it's only half-time, not the end of the game. Things are beginning to look up nationwise. You have to keep the big picture in mind."

"Del saw the big picture," said Swag. "Gave his life to save them kittens for my kids."

"The man understood the broad spectrum of the universality," Puffit said, making another grab for the big brass ring of eloquence.

"You can say that again, Dean," said Swag.

"Del's not dead yet," said Puffit. "But I suppose I owe him an apology on the Ludd thing."

"The shortest distance between two points is an apology," mumbled Spent.

"Shit," Puffit said.

"I'd give my right arm to know who torched that building," Swag said, determined to stay in the conversation.

"Men like that need jobs," said Puffit. "They need the future. I'm not excusing what they did, but we have to remember that they depend on progress as much as you and I. Who's going to put bread on the table if they don't go ahead with this project out here in the dunes? Tearing things up may not look good, but it makes jobs. People forget that."

"I understand she's gonna be a big one—that hole they're talkin' about diggin' out here in the dunes," said Swag to Puffit. He was calm now, his mind momentarily off Dooley and the fire. He was back into his role as dump trucker, front-end loader, owner of a visored cap with "CAT" emblazoned on the crown, a mover and shaker—if only of sand and gravel—a man who knew the difference between a gasket and a bushing, a believer in what machines could do for mankind.

"You're right about that," said Puffit. "That hole will require removal of forty million tons of sand and stone. Of course, seven million tons will go back, as cover over the rad-waste."

"Backfill," said Swag, proud to make a contribution.

Puffit nodded approvingly. "I see you have a good understanding of the technical side of these things."

"I try to keep up with the times."

"The contractors will be using the DOE's Canyonland Basin Plan, the Department of Energy's CBP," Puffit explained. "Actually it's the same plan as the Gibson Dome Project Plan, GDP. That action plan was put together back in the eighties for Utah. A lot of bitching from the environmentalists stalled it until now. The project out here will be called Operation Motherlode. We call it OM for short."

"Sounds like a biggie," said Swag. "Make a lot of changes around here."

"Projects like Motherlode always mean a lot of change. This whole area will be undergoing change," the dean said, his mood dilating at the thought of change.

"For damn sure," said Swag.

"Change is what brought this country along to where it is," said Puffit.

"That is for *damn* sure," Swag repeated.

"Just think of what change has done for this country in the computer field, for instance," Puffit continued. "Take Santa Clara Valley south of San Francisco. It used to be called the Valley of the Heart's Desire. Well, our heart's desire turned out to be computer chips. That entire area of the country has undergone substantial transition in recent years, all the way down to Mexico. Of course, Mexico has been in the transition mode for some years too."

Swag sat forward in his chair. The dean had impressed him with "transition mode."

"For damn sure," he repeated.

Puffit was flattered. He continued, pressing the tips of his fingers together as he talked. "A few years ago, that whole area out there was nothing but marsh, squawking pelicans and orchards. That was about it. Nothing else. Now it's one of the biggest industrial corridors in the world, all tip-up prefab buildings."

"Must be quite a sight," said Swag. "Never got out that way."

"It is. Some, of course, had to be moved up into the hills because of this temporary polar ice-melt thing. But there was nothing in those hills anyway except farms and ranches."

"Computers have brought a lot of change, that's for sure," Swag agreed.

"Hell," said Puffit, "twenty years ago the idea of a three-d computer game in a barroom was just a dream. Now it's an everyday thing. Something we take for granted. Computers mean change, transition."

"I used to think that word *transition* meant going to hell in a handbasket," said Swag. "When a city neighborhood turns into a slum, TV always says it's in transition."

"It's change," said Puffit. "Growth. All very exciting.

'The roaring traffic boom,' as the old song used to say. That sort of thing. It's like the excitement of living near an airport. Something going on all the time."

"Never liked the transition around airports much," said Swag. "Not sure Dorothy will go for living in the transition around Operation Motherlode."

"OM'll tear things up a bit, but it will mean at least three thousand jobs. Three thousand minimum."

"Puttin' things together can make jobs too," said Swag, anxious to keep up with the dean.

"Exactly. But you have to break eggs to make an omelet."

Spent had tried to stay out of the discourse on transition. Transition had just overwhelmed Thistledown. He did not like to think of what it would do to his beloved dunes. But he could not resist a comment. "That's what these hospitals are all about too, Tom—transition. So are funerals." He slumped, eyes closed, into the low-backed chair, his head bent backward awkwardly across the top of it.

Puffit refused to take the bait. He wanted to talk more about making omelets.

This damn conversation's going nowhere, Spent thought. He got up and went out to walk the streets.

Spent's mind drifted back to his father's funeral. He remembered watching the wisps of incense from the swaying censer as it clung about the casket and curled among the gladiolus. He remembered the six tall candlesticks that stood in black, rectilinear finality about the bier as the hollow of his chest tightened around his grief.

"Old Harry passed away, ya know," they said of his father at the local tavern. He heard old Louie Bizek say, "I was up to see him at the funeral home. He didn't look natcheral at all. Seems like nothin' looks natcheral anymore."

And then the lines from George Eliot flooded back into his mind, this time more or less in their entirety... "the growing good of the world is partly dependent on unhistoric acts, and that things are not so ill with you and me as they might have been is half owing to the number who lived faithfully a hidden life and rest in unvisited tombs."

Spent remembered his father laughing in a booming voice around the beer barrel at church picnics, watched him dance a polka, red-faced, perspiring, with a very fat crippled lady named Anna—because nobody else ever danced with Anna—while his mother glowered from the booth where she sold raffle tickets for a handmade quilt that glowed like a setting sun. He remembered how his father gathered a half dozen boys about him and gave them lessons about the design of leaves, ironwood leaves, birch leaves, maple leaves. Even pine needles were called leaves, they found out. And he remembered how Harry would walk down to the creek on the Siegerd farm at four-thirty to bring the cows home for the old man who was slowly dying from too much booze, and how his father pointed toward the haunted spruce swamp to the west where, he said, the Indians gathered moss to stuff the cradleboards that swaddled infant warriors.

At the time, after his father had shown him the sheen on the petals of a buttercup and told him that each petal was handpainted by a medieval troll who still lived, Spent suspected, way back in a crevice on the right side of his young brain, that he would see the world forever as Harry did, and would be banished eternally to a land of chimeras and vagaries, because romantics like his father always seemed to be spending their tenderness as if there were no tomorrow, but mostly because they enjoyed a vagabond spendthrift's caprice rather than the simple act of loving. And he sensed then, too, that he would languish forever in holy exile from common sense.

* * *

Later, as if the sun had burst through leaden clouds of gloom, Dr. Bliss reentered the waiting room, smiling. It was five-thirty in the morning. Bliss rubbed his eyes. He had been catching a wink or two in the doctors' lounge.

"Our patient, Mr. Dooley, has responded marvelously to the new burn sprays we have applied—applied lavishly, of course," he said.

"The lavisher the better," said Swag, happy, suddenly on the verge of tears.

Bliss was apologetic. Dooley was not as bad off as he had implied. "My colleagues did the workup in emergency, you know," he said, "when Mr. Dooley was brought in. I confine myself to advisory work, the public relations side." His head began to tremble. He raised a hand and thumped one side of it as if to drain water from an ear. The trembling stopped.

"Will he be scarred?" asked Spent.

"The only permanent damage was a badly singed pubic section... and his scalp. Neither will grow hair again," the doctor said.

"He ain't married, and he was half-bald already," said Swag. "No big deal."

"May I refer Mr. Dooley to a colleague in Chicago for further work when he is fully recovered—a Dr. Rejoice Benefits?"

Swag took the card, studied it, smiled gratefully and handed it to Spent.

"Dr. Benefits does therapeutic counseling on North Michigan," Bliss said.

"The Gold Coast!" Swag said, still grinning.

"For those fortunate enough to have sustained visible damage to their heads," said the doctor. "Mr. Dooley should respond quickly to the proper toupées. A bit pricey perhaps, but they should do the trick."

* * *

Later that morning, after Puffit and Spent had had breakfast with Dorothy, they journeyed back to Chicago on the South Shore. Spent was intent on seeing Violet. Pester had taken her home the night before, and with Pester around anything could happen to a girl like Vi.

Puffit slept most of the way into town, including through an incident outside Hammond when a band of pickets, protesting layoffs at a furnace factory, attacked the train and broke the windows out of the car behind the one that he and Spent were in. But the train pulled away before more damage could be done, and as far as the commuters were concerned, they were grateful for the senseless violence. It was one of the old, formerly air-conditioned cars with permanently fixed windows. Fresh air cascaded into the car and it felt almost cool again.

CHAPTER 13

The burning of Thistledown plunged Spent into depression, viscid, opaque and bottomless. During the waning months of 1997 he rode the train back and forth to FSU with the enthusiasm of a footsore tortoise. The depths of his despair were evident from his classical symptoms of despondency. He wrote bad poetry, something that had always come rather too easily to him; he watched a lot of television, something he had never found all that difficult; he hung around taverns listening for clues to the meaning of life in the philosophic musings of bar flies, also something toward which he had an easy, natural bent; and he drifted in and out of art museums, which he loved to do, hunting for insights into the peculiar quality of the culture he lived within.

At one point his journals gave birth to a particularly bitter lamentation.

> I study my image in the window of the train. The nose—meant to sniff the rose—runs. The ears—meant to thrill to the gondolier's barcarolle—clog.

> Arteries—meant to surge with the blood of love—
> turn vermicular and varicose. In the mirror, up close,
> life resembles the rectum of a sloth.

Part of the reason for Spent's condition was Violet Fromel. Anselm Pester had taken her home the night of the Thistledown fire and for almost ten days Spent could not reach her. Her brother had headed for Alaska, so he was no help. The Toad had, of course, thrown Violet out of her apartment near the old Windermere.

From the bits and pieces that Violet was willing to reveal to Spent, after she called him and begged him to take her in, which he did, he pieced together a picture of what had gone on. First Pester used the collection of dirty limericks to cast his spell. Like Kay Dooley, Violet discovered that she loved poetry, and while the limericks lacked some of the qualities of Pope or Racine, they spoke of their times and had impact. Then Pester pumped her full of narcotics, alcohol and puke rock. He topped off his assault on her sensibilities by scouring his copy of de Sade's *One-Hundred-and-Twenty Days of Sodom* for small, unambitious sexual prescriptions that he and Violet might work into his scenario for the truly free expression of human aspirations in the nineties.

After a week of such freeform modeling of lifestyles, Violet found an unused element of wholesomeness still very much alive down within her. She told the professor that she had had enough. She told him he was a degenerate creep. He blamed her reaction to his purple recipes on the fact that she was born in North Dakota. He tried to kill her with an omelet pan and she locked herself in the bathroom. She rested there for two days, then stumbled out to the street, hailed a taxicab to the South Shore terminal, called Spent, begged forgiveness and was forgiven, then took the train to Tremont.

At the train station in Tremont, Spent and Violet had a long, heart-to-heart talk. He was still chagrined, he said. He demanded and got an explanation of her infidelity.

The cause of her wayward behavior, Violet said, was vulnerability. Such vulnerability, she reminded Spent, was as important in the nineties as it was in the eighties and it was the one thing a man like Pester was expected to cultivate. It showed itself in the limericks. They spoke of the loneliness and hunger of the free-spirited degenerate. They were not just modish, but post-modish, as moving as anything she'd seen in X-rated movies. Because she was a child of her times she found herself all too terribly vulnerable.

Spent realized from the way Violet was tossing the word *vulnerability* around that she had either been reading Sunday supplement psychology or had been ruined by some high-tech sexual innovation. Pester, in fact, had patented a solar-powered vibrator five or six years earlier. It was hailed at FSU as the kind of technological ingenuity the world could expect from a progressive university faculty. But Spent loved Violet and he needed her desperately. He, after all, was also vulnerable, and though he often tried not to be—telling himself through clenched teeth that what the world now desperately needed were a few people who took pride in their strengths rather than their weaknesses—he found himself sobbing in Violet's arms as she kissed away his vulnerable tears with vulnerable, greedy lips.

Violet moved into the Swagmacher home. After a hurry-up marriage—which Dorothy insisted upon, and the atavism of which Violet attributed to Dorothy's "livin' out here in all this fresh air"—the women were soon as close as sisters. Violet threw away her puke rock makeup kit and Third World pumps, bought a pair of tennis sneakers and undesigned jeans and was quickly caught up in the domestic life of her new home, fussing excitedly over the cooking, caring for Timmy and Kenny as if they were her own, listening enraptured as Swag told Dorothy of his plans for buying a used dump truck to get in on the action of Operation Motherlode.

But something seemed to have gone out of Spent, and the whole thing with Violet left him somewhat flat. He dragged himself to and from work at FSU and in and out of the marriage bed in a distracted way, as if some deeper, all-consuming preoccupation had stolen his heart.

By the time Christmas carolers were out in December of 1997, giant earth movers, drag-line shovels and bulldozers were at work on the new "waste isolation facility system" known as Operation Motherlode. Washington announced with a flourish that digging the massive hole east of Gary would make an enormous economic contribution to the good life in the Midwest. It would provide jobs and it would help renew confidence in the American Way. "We may not be able to build things as big as we used to," said the secretary of energy as he put his foot to the silver-plated shovel that moved the first load of sand from the site, "but if we put our hearts and minds to it we can dig a bigger hole than anyone else, including the Russians or the Chinese!"

As was usual with this sort of thing, Washington requirements for "preplanning" at Motherlode were elaborate, though policy and operation manuals never seemed to say what postplanning might be. They called for stripping away the sand and burying radioactive concrete and steel rubble from decommissioned reactors in the Midwest. But the secretary of energy realized that if a colossal burial site was a good thing, a truly gargantuan site was obviously better. He ordered more preplanning, this to include provision for burying high-level waste containing plutonium. "Americans take pride in things that are high level," he said at the press conference on Motherlode. "Low-level waste burial projects don't do much for anybody's pride!"

The high-level waste was to be contained in cannisters a hundred feet long, built of grout, steel and "overpack laminations." Each cannister was to be buried in a hole bored into the "host rock" laid bare as the sand of the dunes park was stripped back. Since decommissioned fuel rods could reach temperatures of 300 degrees Centigrade, a million and a half gallons of water from Lake Michigan were to be pumped each day over, under and around cells dug in the host rock. The objective was "a disposal system dynamically interfaced with its task environment."

Needless to say, during congressional hearings on Operation Motherlode—which were brief—environmental groups from the Chicago area raised angry questions about site security. Preplanners were quick with reassuring charts and graphs. "High-level radioactive waste has a half-life of one hundred thousand years," said their dulcet-voiced spokesman. "Therefore, our plans contain *explicit, detailed* provision for posting a guard force at the site for one hundred eighty-seven thousand years. During that time the radioactive waste will decay to precisely one-fifth its initial volume. At that point, the guard force will be reduced. Money saved will be promptly earmarked for social programs. Among the programs eligible will be whooping cough inoculations for Caribbean immigrant children and legal counsel for the homeless elderly."

The labor union representatives present at the hearings were particularly impressed with the cogency of this argument. All but the die-hard environmental fanatics were won over.

Work at Motherlode moved fast. A new thirty-mile-long railroad bed was blasted and a new railroad laid from Zion, Rockford and Newsville, Illinois, across the slums of Chicago, through the ruins of the old Dan Ryan Freeway interchanges, across northern Indiana's festering slums and out into the open air of the Dunes National Park. The railroad seemed to be completed almost before it was begun, so rapidly did housing condemnation, acquisition and demolition proceed. By March 1998 the first railcars of radioactive rubble were already parked on sidings near the Motherlode site, large chunks glowing softly in the dark, waiting patiently to come to final rest upon the host rock.

Spent watched the awesome march of progress from the windows of the rickety old South Shore commuter trains. The scene reminded him of drawings he had once seen in *Life* magazine, or perhaps *National Geographic*—he could not remember which—of what seemed like ant armies building the pyramids of the Nile. The countryside was alive with men and machines. Each machine was surrounded by swarms of workmen, some suntanned, some black, all in yellow hardhats. They wore bluejeans and workshoes with bulbous toes. Long hair hung from under the hardhats, snarled, matted with sweat and grime. Some workmen scurried about with red-and-white striped surveying rods, others with shiny black transits. Others dug holes by hand with shovels in preparation for blasting drills. Here and there a geyser of dust erupted as dynamite blasts were set off in the hard subsand and rock. A lot of laughing and joshing went on, even among the riflemen posted about the site to prevent some act of senseless violence. It felt good to work again.

Motherlode was indeed an economic shot in the arm for the Chicago area. By April 1998 eighteen hundred construction workers toiled there. With families, support workers, people in the vending business, fast-food operations, electronic amusement galleries and taverns, the total came to well over six thousand. Some lived in the trailer parks abandoned by steel mill workers after some of the big mills closed in the eighties. Others lived in barracks—variously named Dune Vista, Lake View, Surfside and such—built of prefabricated tip-up walls and roofs shipped in from migrant worker camps surrounding the faltering citrus farms of southern California.

Spent's morale did not improve substantially, even though he was now director of Puffit's UFO Lifestyles Research and Development Center and he had a handsome lettered sign on his door that read "UDOLRADC, Casper Martin Spent, Director." Nor did the awesome march of progress he watched through the windows of the rickety old South Shore trains do much good. He would come home in listless condition, pick at his food, ignore Swag, Dorothy and the kids. And although he tried hard to be a good husband to a wife who had turned out to be a gem, there was something lacking. He would slump with a beer in front of the television set and scarcely utter a word for hours. Violet would sit on the arm of the chair trying to comfort him with neck rubs. But he would watch anything that came on television, which pleased Violet and made no difference to him.

"Twenty-nine seconds and counting. Twenty-eight seconds and counting. Twenty-seven seconds and counting," chanted the advertisement on Spent's television set. A giant new advertising push was on to get people to use a new rectal suppository guaranteed to give soothing relief within thirty minutes.

A pop version of Handel's *Water Music* played over the landscape projected on the screen, a soft John Constable landscape, with a solitary constipate lolling in pinstripe business suit, shepherd's crook in one hand, digital watch in the other, amid a flock of money-colored sheep.

The commercial over, a program announcer said in an enthusiastic yet authoritative voice, "This is EVENT: 1998! Another triumph of the human spirit. A staggering achievement of our scientific community."

Two physicists were about to announce to the world that they had completed calculations begun long ago, in the eighties, to fix precisely the age of the universe. The breakthrough had taken place in laboratories perched atop a mammoth installation buried deep in Morton Salt's Fairport mine outside Cleveland. One of the spin-offs was the taming of the quark, a subatomic particle that was the bottom rung of the ladder of creation. With the quark in harness, the ultimate weapon could be built and man could demonstrate once and for all his prowess as the rational animal.

Since the sixties it had been suspected by some physicists—pessimists, actually—that the proton, the very belly of the atom, was not the Gibraltar of cosmic stability once assumed. There was evidence, said broadcast copy, "that it, too, is vulnerable." Given time, it decayed into light. So experimenters carved a giant cavity the size of a six-story office building out of the Fairport salt bed, lined it with black plastic, filled it with purified water, inserted several thousand highly sensitive photomultipliers and left it in total darkness.

The proton did decay. With the death of each a tiny wink of light, a final *auf wiedersehen* appeared on laboratory computer screens. And when the rate of decay was fixed, scientists were able to count backward to the blinding moment of the universe's creation. Two scientists at work in the Cleveland salt mine, Dr. Arnheim Kauf of Bern and Dr. Renghi Shiva of Bombay, had driven home the golden spike.

Kauf and Shiva faced three big-name television commentators, Ben Someberg of ABC, formerly a football game announcer, Roger Keith-Smithson of BBC, dean of political gossip columnists, and Melissa Krank, anchor of the CBS smash hit, "So You Think You Got It Bad." It was to be a freewheeling discussion, with Krank leading it off with her tough, no-nonsense style. She also had a habit of grinding her sibilants—*s* and *sh*—as only a hard-driving news hawk can.

"Dr. Kauf, according to grand unificashun theory, which we can call GUT for our viewer's convenience, jusht how old is the universh?"

"At eight o'clock this evening, twenty billion three hundred million, four thousand years and twelve minutes, plus or minus four seconds. Our equations will not give us the precise second. Heisenberg's uncertainty principle, you know." Kauf, in business suit, red club tie and loafers, his English flawless, was a model of button-down savoir faire.

"It continuesh to age during this broadcasht, of coursh?" Krank asked rhetorically, eager to demonstrate her grasp of cosmology.

"True."

"Doesh the GUT time frame take ush back to the Big Bang or merely back to the primal particle?"

Kauf coughed slightly. He had been a bit slipshod. Kauf's accent suddenly showed through. "You are kavite correct. To the primal particle, in point of fahct."

"This yoyo has no string, thought Krank. But instead of pressing Kauf, she turned and nodded to Keith-Smithson.

"How large can we say the primal particle was, Dr. Kauf?" asked the Britisher, eager to use "we" rather than "you," experienced newsman that he was, taking a slice of the credit for the scientific leap forward.

"The size of a golf ball," said Kauf.

"British or American?"

Kauf frowned, stuck.

The BBC journalist let Kauf off the hook, or tried to. "The English ball, doctor," he said, "is smaller than the American, for aerodynamic reasons. Winds are customarily stronger on British golf courses. On Sin Andrews, which the Americans pronounce *Saint* Andrews (mild disdain reflexively tightened his upper lip) the wind is several knots . . ."

Ben Someberg, suddenly alert, eager, interjected, "Use a Dunlop Maxfli Ninety, Surlan cover."

Kauf had never heard of Dunlop, or Maxfli, or Surlan cover. He took a chance. "To be sure, Maxfli Ninety. It took ten-to-the-thirty-fourth tenths of a second for the universe to reach dot size."

Krank, intent, businesslike, a hand moving quickly across her chic-short spiked crewcut—the Coconut Look, stylists called it—ever conscious of Nielsen ratings, Dunlop Maxfli or not, said, "And how might we make this point in laymen's termsh? For the man-on-the-shtreet among our viewersh?" The question was a prearranged cue.

Shiva, his dark eyes sparkling, part of the show at last, held up a large cardboard poster. It read:

.000,000,000,000,000,000,000,000,000,000,000,01
of a second

Someberg laughed a belly laugh. "Looks like the rushing average for the New Orleans Saints."

Krank withered him with her famous "You boob!" glance, then asked Kauf, "Doctor, the public wantsh to know what the bottom line ish. What ish it?"

Kauf was up to the challenge this time. No accent now. "Quite simple. We confirmed our calculations while there was still time."

"You mean because of the quark bomb, doctor?"

"Someone will certainly use it, Washington or Moscow—or Tripoli."

"And then?"

"Our funding sources will have dried up."

A small, desperate groan rose from Spent. "Should have never turned the damn thing on," he said absentmindedly to Violet. *"Mea maxima culpa."* He reached out with his foot and pushed the television off-button.

"I need some air, honey, and time to think," he said as he got out of his chair, put on his shirt and headed for a tavern called Childe Harold's, which wasn't far from where Operation Motherlode was in full swing. The tavern was owned by Harold Sims, a small, darkly handsome man of thirty-five or so. He had taken a Ph.D. in eighteenth-century poetry, but was never able to find work in a school system or survive on his writing. So he bought an old grocery store at the intersection of Waverly Road and Highway 12 and converted it into a bar that catered to Motherlode workers.

Despite the optimism that bloomed in the wake of Operation Motherlode, doubt continued to haunt the minds of many of the workmen. They had heard about the hazards of working around radiation, but when these anxieties were expressed at Childe Harold's there was always someone to put the doubter in his place.

That happened when a railroad switchman responsible for shunting the carloads of radioactive rubble onto the tracks of the marshalling yards complained that he sometimes felt nauseated after a long day's work. A man at the bar said that it would take a lot more than something nobody could see to frighten him, and he laid a ten-dollar bill on the bar. He said he would bet it and anything anyone else in the place could come up with that he could eat a wineglass. He would eat razor blades, too, if he was challenged with enough money.

Twenty dollars appeared on the bar, then thirty-five. Sims found a wineglass and set it up before the man. He ate it, stem, bowl, the works, drawing a varied response from his audience. One big bruiser covered his ears with his hands. The railroad man said the sound of the glass eater made him sick. He went into the lavatory and threw up; others cheered.

"Well, bars always did attract men who live exciting lives," said Sims. "Isn't it something what people can do when they decide to use their God-given talents?"

The glass eater pocketed the money, ordered a new stein of beer and drank it down without taking the mug from his lips, his elbow high, a man's man all the way.

"A man can eat glass if he wants to," said one of the skeptics in the group, "but this here radiation thing ain't as easy on a man as a little broken glass. Ground-up glass will pass right through a man, like sand. Glass is sand. I know, I worked in a bottle factory. Saw sand turn into glass lots of times. But radiation don't pass through like sand would. Stays inside you somehow. More like swallowing a spoonful of this here industrial enamel they're using on some of them new buildings at Mother. It'll coat your insides and then just stay there."

The glass eater was not impressed with the theory of enameled intestines. "Take a hell of a lot more'n a few damn waves of some kind to make this fella sick," he said, with all the authority he could muster.

"I know what you're sayin', Sam," said another workman. "You and I agree with them scientists on that one. Radiation is like smokin'. You can show that people get sick more often when they smoke than when they don't smoke, but you sure as hell can't prove it *makes* them sick. And you take these other diseases goin' around, like that epidemic that's killin' so many people in Bulgaria and around there."

The glass eater interrupted. "Well, them people never did stay very clean to begin with. You gotta remember that, Lou."

Lou, a bit annoyed at the interruption, continued. "Know

what they could do to put an end to them epidemics? Less tilt on the earth's axis. Shorter winters. Mean healthier lives for most all of us. 'Cause it would cut down the hibernation time of them rats that carry so many of them diseases. I heard a scientist the other night on television. He said the Bulgaria disease was carried by rodents, rats mostly. Too much time, he said, for them rodents to fuck up a storm down in their burrows in the winter. They overbreed, then get lice and such. Whole thing caused by the tilt of the planet. This scientist says we got rocket power enough to straighten the planet out so they wouldn't have so much time to fuck." The epidemiologist laughed. "Course, the scientist didn't say they was fuckin'. He said they was *copulatin'.*"

Sam was disdainful of Lou's gullibility. "Hell, we got no seasons now."

Lou sputtered, finished his beer and ordered another with a shot of whiskey on the side, top-shelf whiskey, to even the score with Sam.

"Well, hell," said a man named Lem, standing next to Lou, "You can't pick up the damn paper without someone tellin' you that this or that or some damn thing is gonna kill you. I figure there's good and bad in everything. It's like cigarettes. I been smokin' almost twenty years. Ain't dead yet, and I damn well don't intend to die of cigarettes. I smoked when I was a kid. Smoked corn silk when I was in first grade. Learned to use dried red-and-white clover by the time I was six."

"Learned to play with yourself about the same time, didn'tcha Lem?" said Lou, bumping him with his elbow.

"Well, I learned a lot when I was young. Learned about the good and bad in things. Learned smokin' from Billy Thomas, kid I grew up with. But poor Billy, he learned the hard way. His old man was a farmer, mean sonofabitch. Used to leave a leather strap soakin' in the water trough in the barn so he could use it on Billy at the end of the day. Always found something to whip the kid for. And Billy got a little squirrely from it. We used to pick potato bugs off the little garden back of their house, 'cause the old man was too stingy to pay for bug spray. We'd walk up and down the rows and pick potato worms off and drop them into a can of kerosene. Billy would watch them worms wiggle, then for no good reason pick some off the spuds and squeeze them slowly in between his fingers. He called it 'executin' them.' He'd get kinda excited, and dance around and yell. Grew up to be a mean bastard. Killed his wife with a garden rake. Coroner said he tried to rake her eyes out. Bein' mean is a disease too. That's one reason some people want a war. Mad at your old man? Bomb the shit out of them poor bastards livin' in felt boots in Siberia."

"Lot of men got streaks like that in them," said Lou. "Cruel to animals for the same reason. Saw that a few years ago up in the Michigan Peninsula. Pulled up to this filling station. A customer and his wife was standing there looking at a sign on top of a used refrigerator, near this guy's messy little office. Sign said, 'FORTY DOLLARS AS SHE IS. I WILL PUT THE FIRST SIX-PACK IN!'

"In the garage they had a big wooden crate, sides four feet high, covered with chicken wire. A black bear was cooped up inside. There was a small hole on one side, just big enough for the animal to get his head out. That was so it could drink soda pop. Owner trained it to drink Orange Crush through that hole. Swear to God! That animal would whine and twist around and put a big ugly grin on its face. Had huge yellow teeth and a long pink tongue. I can remember how that couple talked:

"'It's a good buy, Ben. You can *see* that,' she says.

"'I can't see puttin' out forty clams,' he says.

"'But our icemaker don't *work* no more,' she says.

"'Well, if *he* comes down five or ten,' he says.

"'You ask him when he gets the car filled with gas. Go *ahead.* Don't be afraid,' she says.

"'You can sure *work* on a man, Gladys,' he says.

"'Work on you something special tonight, Ben,' she says whisperin'.

"Then the kids, two of 'em, start squealing 'cause the bear has got his head through that hole. The old man gave them each fifty cents and they bought Orange Crush. Then he coughed up the money for the refrigerator. The wife runs over and starts huggin' the kids and the bear slobbers all over her coat sleeve. 'Get that dirty thing out of here!' she yelled, and kicked it right in the face. The bear whined like hell from inside the box.

"The gas jockey says, 'That animal sure is a burden. I spend more time on him than you can imagine. And he ain't worth it. He really ain't. Them beasts ain't got a shred of gratitude. 'Course, that's what makes them animals, I suppose. Shoulda never taught that thing to drink orange pop. Never shoulda. Get nothin' back at all. Ain't many bear left, and this bum spends all his time whinin'. I might just let him loose, whether he likes it or not.'"

"People all suffer from tendencies," said Spent ruefully to no one in particular. He had recalled the bronze plaque at old FSU.

Sims loved Spent's drollery. "Show me a man that doesn't suffer from tendencies," he said, "and I'll show you a closet compulsive."

At which point, a big, burly, redheaded man in greasy gray overalls came through the door. His wife, small, pimply faced, grinning without reason, followed like a well-trained house pet.

"My name's Red," he said, holding out his hand to Spent, then to Sims and another customer sitting two stools down the bar from Spent. "Some people call me Speed.

'Cause I drive fast. Don't know where the Red got started... 'cause I'm redheaded, I guess. I don't mind. I like Red, but I like Speed better."

There were handshakes and hellos in return.

"This here is my wife Peanut," he said, introducing the woman.

There were more handshakes and hellos.

"I suppose you all heard about that hangin' in Memphis last week? Peanut and I came through there. Was in all the papers. Nailed that night cutter deader than hell. Got two southeast of Saint Louie, too."

Speed was referring to the public reaction to a new industry that had sprung up, first in the South and then in the North. It was the midnight pirating of logs from cemeteries. During the heyday of the great American lumber barons, when Wisconsin, Michigan, Minnesota, and then Washington and Oregon were logged off, American cemeteries, in particular cemeteries of Confederate and Union dead, were planted with seedlings and small saplings, spindly little things put along cemetery drives or at the head of family plots. By 1998, unnoticed, these trees had matured to hundred-and-thirty-year-old beauties, thick, heavy, pure and hard as granite... oak, maple, cherry and hickory. Suddenly the finest growths of virgin forest in America were to be found in cemeteries—an irresistible lure to the entrepreneurial spirit that had made such names as Weyerhauser household synonyms for dynastic power.

The first raids on cemeteries took place in the old South. The lumbermen did not attempt to dismantle the trees from the top to spare what was on the ground. They simply hacked and power-sawed them down. They fell willy-nilly, battering and bashing gravestones, mausoleums and generals on pedestals as they thudded to the ground.

A half-dozen Confederate graveyards were desecrated

before Dixie honor rebelled. Near Chattanooga a pair of cutters were caught and beaten in one cemetery. Outside Memphis the full force of southern tradition was brought to bear. A cutter was caught, castrated and then hanged.

The effect of the southern response was to move the night cutter industry northward. There the values of "resource harvesting" were well established and far more potent than concern for Confederate graveyard sculpture. Yankee grade-school textbooks referred to the "harvesting of the bison" during the nineteenth century. Some even referred to the "final harvesting of the passenger pigeon in 1914." What incensed most northerners was that the miserable midnight cutters showed no appreciation for the principles of orderly resource harvesting. Once the notion of selective cutting rather than clear cutting was put in place, they argued, the whole thing could be turned to national benefit. But that legislation did not come soon enough to help the fellow lynched in Memphis nor, for that matter, those who were kneecapped in southern Illinois soon after.

"'Course, I seen that kind of thing myself," said Speed. "There's times when you ain't got no choice but to kill a man deader than a damn stone. Had that happen up north a few years ago. I was livin' near Sault Ste. Marie, long-haulin' from Duluth across the bridge to Detroit. This bastard gets drunk and shoots a man in a bar outside Hancock."

Peanut brightened, squeezed Speed's arm. "Tell 'em, honey. Tell the nice men about that jerk Cully."

"Well, they deputized a bunch of us from around town," Speed began, "the ones that did the most huntin' and shot good. We went after that bastard Cully Benson and chased him to swamp country. He was headin' for Lake Kewani. We knew that. It made sense. He could steal a boat and then get lost in those islands and hole up in a shack. But they spotted him at the Whitetail Lodge trying to get a boat. Run him into the woods. Then the mosquitos and ticks worked on him. So he broke into a cottage just a little ways down from the lodge. We could see with the binoculars that the door was broke open. So we hollered at him to come out or we would riddle the place. When he came out, we just unloaded on him. He staggered about five feet. That's a fact. Only five feet. We shot him so full of holes he looked like a sieve. And the dummy didn't even have the damn shotgun they said he had. That's how stupid a guy like that can be.

"Look. I got this here clipping from the newspaper in Sault. They had a news guy with us, like a war correspondent. He took this picture. Eight men with rifles there. It was the reporter's idea for a couple of the men to put their foot on Cully's chest. Them news guys like history.

"Set the table, bartender," said Speed. With a wave of the hand, "Give everybody a drink." Then, to Sims in a loud whisper, "Have a jolt too, Hal, on me. It'll do you good."

Speed folded the photo carefully and put it into his billfold. "Yup," he said to himself with a smile, "we got that bird good. He ain't gonna do no more killin'."

Spent, a cold sweat on the back of his neck, careened to the door and into the night.

As solemnly as a bishop climbing the steps at Chartres on Easter Sunday, Casper Spent walked up the great, white marble staircase of the Chicago Art Institute. He stopped briefly, as if he might genuflect, before the second-century Aphrodite standing there, her shoulder, waist and thigh tracing a line so pure it left men like Ingres permanently hypnotized. He moved to Rodin's great *Burgher,* and thanked a Mrs. A. M. H. Ellis for it. Then past Matisse's

Slave. He blushed. The pecker was polished to a shine by a thousand furtive fingertips.

A clutch of schoolchildren bubbled by, following their teacher-mother hen. They unfolded folding chairs and sat before one of Robert Hubert's great paintings of Roman ruins, and wondered why the goats did not fall off the aqueduct.

Spent reached the Harry Manaster Room, a gracious contribution from another good old Harry, back in 1959. "Where is Harry now?" Spent found himself asking a passerby. Dizzy, vertiginous at the thought of where most Harrys went, he settled into an antique armchair on a platform in the center of the room. It was carved and gilded walnut, a Louis XV piece.

"Get off there, you lout!" shouted a guard who suddenly rounded the corner, his brow curled in an angry frown, his eyes hurling thunderbolts. "Can't you read?" The card read, *These chairs are intended for* courant *use, not for* meublant *use.* Spent slunk away like a cur that had been whipped, then kicked.

And there was Rembrandt! The *Officer With a Gold Chain,* haughty and magnificent, next to poor, poor Christ. Which was the master of the shadow? Which demanded fast footwork, keeping your guard well up, training in shadow boxing? He got no answers from Caravaggio or de la Tour. They could fell a man with a single uppercut of light. And when the gaping gallerygoers eyed Spent, throwing punches in the center of the room, they understood him with nervous, patronizing smiles.

In Gallery 23, Spent took a right on the chin from Delacroix, as a great war horse snorted against a vast red sky. Spent went down for a nine-count.

"Really, sir!" said the astonished guard standing over him. "Are you all right?" He was as solicitous as some runt circling in the ring, courtesy of the Illinois Boxing Commission.

"Yes," said Spent, "but my seconds have suggested a glass of wine." Spent went downstairs to the cafeteria. He bought a small bottle, twisted off the plastic cap and downed the wine. Then he ate two hotdogs with mustard and returned to the galleries, the mustard still smarting on his chin.

He entered the gallery where Lucas Cranach's spirit hung as grand and real as if he were hiding in the corner in a reliquary. The stillness of Sebastian Sheel's *Madonna and the Saints With Child* wrapped the room in peace. There were bluebirds sitting on the fence behind the saints, behind Barbara, Ursula, Agatha, Agnes, Margareta and Apollonia. *Raptus, raptus.* And the tadpole eyes of the old man-baby Jesus stared at him. So did the eyes of the guard, but not as tenderly.

Suddenly he was back in the ring and Monet was swarming all over him. Monet was a slugger. Must have put a lot of time in pitching hay, thought Spent, bobbing, weaving. He bounces light off those stacks as boldly as if they were his supernatural lily pads. Then Renoir climbed into the ring. What a team! "So it's tag wrestling now!" yelled Spent. And there were Renoir's glorious nudes, their billowing thighs like foothills to paradise. Then the lady with the child. Spent had always loved her, married though she apparently was. She looked at Spent, her eyes soft and ethereal.

"I surrender to you all!" Spent bellowed. The echo of his voice reverberated through the galleries and into the atrium. The guard took his arm, squeezing it as if to reduce Spent to a single, giant contusion, and ushered him out of the galleries. "Perhaps you might enjoy the souvenirs," he said, and sent Spent crashing toward the gift shop.

Spent bought ten postcards of the masters, went outside

and sat next to one of the great lions on the steps and listened to the color on those tiny replications explode like heated paint cans inside his brain.

With the changing of the guards, Spent paid his four dollars over again and went back into the galleries. To get to the bottom of things.

At the door he was handed a printed notice. "Performance Art by Bertoline, Priestly Gallery: 5 P.M." Spent headed for the Priestly Gallery, through the great *G* corridor, its hundreds of pedestals empty (an exhibit was on the move), past the room of marvelous paperweights, past the modern Americans, past McCracken's *Red Plank,* past blown-up tears from comic books, past Frankenthaler's yellow blotch with Magic Marker smear, past Oldenburg's big, lonely bronze *Clothes Pin,* past the postminimalist constructionist gallery with its tiny bits of this and that in a large empty room, past the great Trading Room of the Chicago Stock Exchange, a dead temple given as a gift, its column capitals glittering with golden profanity. All but a sarcophagus for greed was missing.

How the people hurry through this emptiness, thought Spent. There are no saints here, no big-eyed infant saviors, no voices, no *raptus,* just a long, unending tunnel walled with sticky solipsism.

"The underlying principle of this installation is one of joyful promiscuity," read the performance handout. In two large rooms the floors were covered with debris from toilets, broken water closets, broken soap dispensers, pieces of copper tubing, cardboard rolls from which the toilet paper was gone, shards of broken tile, torn shower curtains, cracked soap dishes, remnants of bars of soap (in white, brown and beige varieties), empty aspirin and fingernail polish bottles (in shades of red), broken Schick injector razors, broken Norelcos, a cornucopia of detritus, so to speak, from the American bathroom culture. The rubbish was arranged by the "laws of chance." A narrow pathway was cleared through the junk and painted vermillion. It ended in a large black stain. "Is the vermillion path the birth canal? Is the stain the void?" asked the reverent printed commentary.

Mr. Bertoline entered from the right. He was shirtless and hairless. His torso was smeared with pink Vaseline. A camera was mounted above his head on a small boom and powered by batteries. As the hushed gallery of art lovers gathered about, Bertoline lay down and wriggled toward the stain.

A partner or aide, a young he/she, chanted "Red rover, red rover, let the whole thing be over!" as Bertoline struggled toward the void. And he in response moaned again and again, "I have been sent among men to bore them."

The performance took an hour. When Bertoline reached the black stain he was offered a Coke, which he sat up and drank, perspiring, in what appeared to be some misery. The oak floor had been an unforgiving birth canal, and both his knees and elbows had taken a beating. But the camera on his head had preserved his every anguish for the museum's growing library of performance conceptualists. Even the empty soda bottle, lying on its side in the void, was carefully photographed.

Spent, angry now and desperate, his head spinning, stood and shuffled through the rubbish. "Now I rearrange this nihilism. I rearrange it by the laws of chance!" he shouted. Then, as if to answer himself, he yelled, "Chance is a law?" Glaring at the audience he screamed back, "Then so is your goddamned degeneracy." Spent heard the whinny of his unicorn.

A cheer went up. Smiles all around him grew. Many were a deep, dark way-out blue, from chewing betel nut, the latest fashion in New Performance gallerygoing. Spent was now part of the performance, part of the larger conception. He had won a measure of immortality. His eyes wide, his breath heaving, he ran to the nearest wall and with his ballpoint pen scribbled Tertullian's third-century plea to God, "I believe! Help my unbelief!"

The museum curator of performance art rushed up to Spent. "Magnificent!" he cried. He pumped Spent's arm with congratulations. He vowed he would have the scribbled message framed on the wall, as is. He demanded that Spent name his price and begin again, across the hall, anywhere, even across a dead masterpiece or two, perhaps beginning with El Greco's *Assumption of the Virgin,* which he said bored young people anyway. But that would take a ladder since the painting was a big damn thing. If Spent would wait, he would run down to the janitor's quarters to see if he could find a ladder.

It was then perhaps that something snapped in Spent, as the phrase goes. He refused to accept the commission, refused to accept the fame, refused to enter the gallery ever again. "I refuse! I refuse! I refuse!" he mumbled as he rode the train to Tremont in a daze.

And that night, as he tossed in restless sleep, his continued "I refuse!" was taken by Violet to mean she was not welcome in his arms. She wept silently next to him as he snored for almost an hour.

CHAPTER 14

For a few weeks after Spent's encounters with Dr. Kauf, Mr. Bertoline and the like he seemed to recover his equilibrium. He appeared, in fact, to be a paragon of good sense, judicious to the point of tedium. But Delbert Dooley, whom Spent began to see regularly again on the commuter train, detected more than a little to worry about in his friend. Spent seemed more preoccupied and more withdrawn than usual. At first he assumed that Spent was still smarting from Violet's affair with Pester, probably cooking up some scheme to even the ledger. As far as Dooley was concerned, Pester deserved what was coming to him. If Spent beat the tar out of him, or had it arranged, that would suit Dooley just fine. It would be sensible violence in the very best tradition. But it soon became obvious that there was more to it than that.

On one occasion Dooley found Spent in such a gloomy mood that he tried to perk him up by setting up one of the little games of banter that Spent seemed to enjoy so much. It was to be a take-off on a lunatic talking with his lunatic shrink.

"You be the patient, Cass. I'll be the shrink. Call me Dr. Borderline." Dooley had just read a Sunday supplement on the so-called borderline neurosis. It was big business in psychiatry in the nineties, as it had been in the eighties. "I'll use your first name, as if we were close. A little white lie to put my patients at ease."

Spent perked up a bit. "Start with a golden oldie, Del. Ask me a loaded question that's unfair to both of us."

"Harrumph. Do I have the impression, Casper, that you have a feeling of impending doom?"

"The end is nigh."

"You have an anal fixation, Casper."

Spent laughed. He seemed to come out of the haze for a moment. "It's these goddamn wicker seats, doctor."

"Your discomfort is deep-seated?"

"All the way up to the transverse colon."

Dooley began to laugh. Things were pepping up.

"Borderline is where it's at in therapy these days. Rich pickings right along the social fence, under the old post-and-rail we once called psychopathy."

Dooley laughed again, louder. The post-and-rail allusion was pure Spent. Madness, shrinks, rich pickings. And the post-and-rail line added Americana.

But Spent collapsed into seriousness again. "Do you think our lives are as tragic as a zoo?"

Dooley wondered if Spent hadn't slipped over the edge. "Zoo?"

"For the other creatures, Del. The only ones that are making it are those in zoos. It's evidently a choice between prison and extinction. I wonder what our zookeeper will be like? Maybe God is just a zookeeper."

Dooley was not the kind of person to stuff his head into the sand, and he knew it was touch-and-go now with Spent. He decided he would put the best construction on things. There was not much point in adding to Spent's burden by agreeing with him.

"You ought to talk to somebody, Cass," he said, gently, although he did not know to whom. Certainly not the psychiatrist Dooley had seen after Kay walked out on him. All he came away with was a deep distrust of anyone who used words like *love* and *honesty* too freely.

"Well, you're the only one I can talk to, Del."

A lump formed in Dooley's throat.

"Violet's a wonderful woman, but she thinks my new job in research and development at FSU is a dream come true. She always wanted to be a faculty wife, she says. Wants to buy a samovar and have the other wives in. I didn't know she even knew what a samovar was."

There was a long pause. Violet Fromel at the samovar was an image Dooley needed time to work through.

"Do you know what's wrong with our fellow man?" Spent asked abruptly. "It's *Pollyanna pygmantosa.*"

Dooley tried to salvage things with some more fun. "A high-tech implant will cure anything, Casper. New wave, new vision." He was trying to think like Spent, trying to stay in the ballgame, if only for his friend's sake.

"Can new eyes be given to dead souls?" Stillness settled over the conversation again.

Dooley felt helpless. He had grown to like Spent a lot even if Spent's mind remained an enigma to him. But in a way he liked that, too. It reminded him of the old, ornate, one-of-a-kind alarm clock he had once owned. Dooley had dropped the clock accidently. From then on its hour hand would lie dormant for days, then begin running twice as fast as it was supposed to. And its alarm would go off unaccountably early in the late afternoon, as if to warn its owner of approaching night. Dooley kept it around for years just to wonder at its mysterious telos. It was Kay who made him throw it out. She said it was silly-looking and so old-fashioned she was embarrassed for her friends to see it on their front-room shelf.

Spent said, "They say we live in an age of anxiety. But anxiety is nothing but doubt. And doubt is nothing but privation of habit, as someone said."

"I suppose so, Casper."

"Doubt may not be the mother of madness, but it is a brother."

There was another long pause. Spent continued. "Habit is the great gyroscope of nature. We miss our ancient habits." After a moment he added, "Duty, honor, earth."

And when Dooley informed Spent that he was going to move south, to live in the countryside around Bloomington somewhere because he could not watch what was happening to the dunes, Spent felt it as a personal blow, almost a betrayal. He had been toying with the idea of a genuine New Ludd movement.

"At least you have a job here," Spent said, hoping to somehow make a case.

"You have a job here too, Cass."

Spent was cut, but he only asked, "What will you do? How will you support yourself?"

"I'll do some woodwork, furniture. I'll have my own patch of land. Maybe Kay will come down after a while."

"I'll miss you. I'll miss you a lot."

Dooley had been unable to look at Spent. He looked out the window and made a comment about the weather.

Spent again tried hanging around taverns, but that didn't work. The thought of a career in performance art left him cold. He had had it with watching television. He began taking long walks alone at night. He would lie on one of the great dunes well east of Motherlode and stare at the sky. Each time a space platform hove into view he would roll over and hug the earth until the gleaming atrocity was out of sight. Then the sky would be clean again, sewn with a million seeds of light, Cygnus, Cassiopeia, Hercules, draped by the ancient imagination across the shoulders of man's first wonderment. Only in this age of science, he thought, have we filled the heavens with flying objects we either hate or cannot identify.

At eleven o'clock on one of those nights of wonder, Spent was shot. He had been sitting high on one of his favorite dunes watching excavators below him. The great shovels worked under giant floodlights. They chugged and heaved themselves about like huge beetles devouring a hunk of decaying meat. With each load they dug from the wall of the excavation an avalanche of sand would slide to the bottom of the yawning hole.

Spent was composing poetry by pocket flashlight. Like most of his poetry in recent months, it was heavy with rhyme, answering to a primitive demand for predictability that pounded in his head. The poetry did not clear his mind. It did the reverse. Its doggerel lowered a cooling mist of sentiment over the seething jungle world in which his half-formed desire to act had wandered, lost and pathetic, for so long.

A small white oak tree near where Spent was sitting toppled suddenly into the Motherlode gorge. He became hysterical.

"Madmen," he shrieked. "Whores from hell! Criminals!" he shouted, sliding and tumbling down the slope toward the shovel nearest him. When he reached the bottom he raced to the great machine, climbed the ladder to its operator's cabin, tore open the door and threw himself on the operator. The worker was a young man of twenty, powerful as a bull. He punched Spent once in the face and sent him twisting, doing a kind of slow-motion somersault to the ground. The shovel operator called the guards on his dashboard intercom.

Spent had not been seriously hurt. He pulled himself to his feet and started to run. He seemed, the guard said later, to be heading for a dynamite shed near the thicket of dead trees and brush that littered the east wall of the excavation. The guard shot once in the air, then at Spent. The bullet hit him somewhere in the back and he spun about. He went down to one knee, then rose and scuttled into the tumbled litter of trees and brush.

The guards were unable to find Spent, who dragged himself back to the top of the dig and went home. Only Violet was there. Swag had taken Dorothy and the kids to an outdoor movie in Chesterton to celebrate a raise he had gotten as one of the truck drivers at Motherlode.

Spent staggered into the house and collapsed on the living room floor. Violet held his head in her lap, cradling him, swaying, weeping. "I've called the ambulance, honey. Don't worry none."

"I'm shot, Violet," he said. "I've been shot by a human being."

"Don't fret, honey. You'll be all right. I looked at where you was shot. You won't die."

Spent smiled faintly. "Say something about man's capacity to endure," he said. "It's in all the books."

She smoothed a hand across his face. Her hand was cool. He thought of those times when he was only eight, tunneling in the January drifts that formed behind the little tool shed of his father Harry, where the raspberry canes acted like a snow fence. The wind from the northwest would sweep around the little shed and the snow would harden, layer upon layer until it was strong enough for him to walk on. It was ideal for tunneling. He would burrow into the drift and then cut out a maze of secret chambers. He would cut the roof so thin the light shone through and he could hear the wind. He would lie there on his back licking the snow from his mittens, and the odor of the wet wool of his stocking cap would mix exuberantly with the white of that blessed underworld.

The smile returned to Spent's face. "Say something about reaffirmation, Vi," he said. "That's in all the best books too."

"Shhhh." She leaned over, kissing him.

Spent reached down and touched his backside. When he drew his hand up it was wet with blood. "Red is not the color of life, Violet. It is the color of our undoing. It is the color of passion, fire and pain. The perfect world would be a world gone utterly white."

"Yes, I understand," said Violet, though she hadn't a clue and thought that Spent was hallucinating.

"I see a trumpeter swan, Violet," he said. "They're not all gone. I hear it." There was a distant look in her husband's eyes.

"Sure you do, darling. And it's all right. The ambulance will be here any minute."

"Am I bleeding, Violet?" he asked.

"Just a little. You'll be all right. I think I hear the ambulance siren," she said.

"I'm in your lap, dear. I'm in the lap of fortune."

"Shhhh."

The swan was circling high above the earth. Both the bird and the planet seemed weary. The great bird circled and circled again. It was far out at sea, above a place where its island had once been. It turned into the wind and toward the east. The ocean glowed as if afire. It was dawn, or perhaps some terrible fever.

The swan drifted down the sky, awash in breeze as sweet and insubstantial as its memory. Then slowly the world began to unwind. Heaven lost its horizon, and the sky began to evaporate.